Stay the Night

STAY THE NIGHT

For more information, to inquire about rights to this or other works, or to purchase copies for special educational, business, or sales promotional uses please write to:

The Zharmae Publishing Press, L.L.C.
5638 Lake Murray Blvd, Suite 217
La Mesa, California 91942
www.zharmae.com

FIRST EDITION

Published in Print and Digital formats in the United States of America

The golden Z logo, and the TZPP logo are trademarks of
The Zharmae Publishing Press, L.L.C.

ISBN: 978-1-937365-87-5

10 9 8 7 6 5 4 3 2 1

Stay the Night

Kathleen McMahon Schwartz

Zharmæ

Seattle | Las Vegas | San Diego | Los Angeles | Spokane

Thank you to my husband for his patience, my writers groups for their encouragement, and the Stowe Free Library for those free writers workshops.

Stay the Night

Chapter 1

Bent over with my butt in the air, blood filling my head and breathing like an overworked ox, I was dripping sweat, wringing out my tension. Anika, my svelte and encouraging yoga teacher, pressed down on my lower back, trying to tweak my down-dog position. "Relax, Maureen; breathe, breathe, sitz bones higher."

Well, I pushed my sitz bones higher, all right, and fired off a shotgun blast! I froze with embarrassment. I could no longer relax or breathe. When class ended, I rolled up my mat and slipped past my yoga buddies, knowing my face was covered in red blotches: an irritating part of my Irish heritage.

Exercise was my fountain of youth, or so I hoped. At sixty-nine, I watched as acquaintances sucked, tucked, lasered, or surgically lifted every visible body part. I did feel some pride in not spending the thousands of bucks those procedures cost, but I put in many hours with weights, yoga, and Pilates with the same farcical hope. Even with my devotion to working out, all my fat cells seemed to have migrated to my stomach.

I joined my best friend, Susan Katz, at our pool, the centerpiece of the Ocean Gardens senior condo complex. Bodies in bright, hopeful swimwear were lounging around or bobbing on noodles in the water. Most folks looked over seventy, many over eighty. I averted my eyes to avoid viewing the effects of gravity.

Susan looked up at me from her chaise longue and frowned. "You look stressed. Thought your yoga stuff is supposed to relax you, no?"

I dropped into a chair and let out a sigh. "Yeah, but I let another one rip today—in the same class. I'm never going back."

"But you love yoga. And that's why they call us old farts." Susan started to laugh—at me. "You know it's probably all that healthy stuff you eat. Just cut down on veggies and woodchip cereal." By that point she was actually guffawing. "I'd probably blast off to the moon on your crunchy diet."

"This is serious, Sue." I tried not to laugh.

For a break, I jumped into the pool and did laps until my arms were numb with exhaustion. When I staggered back and sat down, Susan poked me. "You're missin' the show," she said, flicking her eyes toward the pool's deep end. "Look at Mildred, flirting and showin' off those wrinkled boobs."

We watched the submerged lovebirds—Leo Silverman, our seventy-something Romeo, with his newest conquest. As the two ascended the pool steps, holding hands, Susan and I exchanged a "yuck."

Leo strolled by us—still gripping Mildred's hand—and gave me a musical "Hello, Maureen" and a big wink.

I returned a curt nod. *What nerve!*

Susan was giggling, almost gagging. "Well, I think our old playboy likes you, Reenie. Didn't he ask you out last month?"

"Yup. The big-spender asked me out for coffee. Three times! He doesn't give up. Told him I'm still in mourning."

"Well, I think it's time you pulled yourself together, *bubala*. It's been over two years since John died. I know he was the love of your life, but you gotta enjoy these golden years."

"I enjoy my life, I do. Just don't want an old man in it. And look who's talking. You never even married."

"Not many men look twice at me, hon. But you've always had them sniffin' after you like gators in heat. In college, you had to beat them off with your slide rule."

My interest in men and sex had evaporated when my husband, John, died two years ago. Actually, it was killed off long before. John had a prostate operation six years before he passed, and even with Viagra and Cialis, he never could perform again—his attempts were like trying to stuff a marshmallow up a nostril.

I shook off my reverie. "Listen. I got a scary email from Alyssa early this morning. Said she had to talk to me tonight, 'very serious,' but…I don't know. She never calls."

Susan's eyebrows knitted together. "She probably needs to 'borrow' from you again. Something's not right with our gal."

Susan loved my daughter as much as I did, but Alyssa no longer had time for us. At twenty-seven, she was a successful freelance animator; I made all my friends watch her dancing cell phones on TV and bragged to everyone that her animated Mini Cooper ads won industry awards. John and I had sacrificed to send her to Pratt, but we rarely saw our beautiful daughter once she reached college. Alyssa acted like our home in New Jersey was light-years away from Brooklyn. She always had excuses for avoiding us.

"Sorry, Mom. I can't get home for Thanksgiving. Got a big project due."

"Listen, Alyssa. We're only two hours away, and you know Dad is very ill. Please make an effort. We both miss you."

"Sure. I'll try to get there. And I'll call Dad if I can't make it."

***

During her college years we knew John was dying—each month another part of him ebbed away—so my reactions to Alyssa's avoidance were drowned out by my misery. It was her freshman year at Pratt when our worlds were knocked out of orbit. On a rainy September morning, John said, "Can you come with me to the doctor's tomorrow?"

A spark of fear ran through me. "What's up, hon?"

His voice was hoarse and his eyes filled with tears. "I get some test results back tomorrow— it's probably gonna show cancer."

John—tough John, my man of tools who could build anything— never cried.

"No! And even if it does, they can fix anything today." The shock of hearing someone you love might have cancer wipes every other thought out of your mind. We cried together that afternoon and many other afternoons to come.

John had kept his series of appointments and tests a secret. Now it all spilled out: a high PSA blood test, an embarrassing ultrasound up the anus, a painful biopsy. I listened to the litany of his escalating fright.

The next day we sat across a wide expanse of desk, holding hands and peering at Dr. Drummond, who was almost hidden by computer monitors. The doctor coughed, then spoke. "Mr. Manning, I'm afraid the biopsy was positive. We'll need to run more tests, but I expect you'll need a radical prostatectomy as soon as possible. Do either of you have any questions?"

Any questions! Hundreds of questions. My mouth was too dry to speak that day. John's life was taken over by tests, MRIs, CTs. We got a second opinion (I hated Dr. Drummond) but both doctors concurred. After the surgery, John and I listened to his death sentence. The cancer had spread and there was no treatment for metastasized prostate cancer—just some ugly drugs that could slow things down.

I remembered taking John to the ritzy Short Hills Mall two years before he died. In the middle of a crowded, sunlit concourse, he'd let out a moan while urine ran out of him, staining his pants, dripping onto the marble floor. I still felt guilty for wanting to leave him in his puddle and run. No wonder I had so little time for Alyssa then.

***

By late afternoon, I was napped and groomed, my freshly-highlighted hair glowing, and wearing a new T-shirt that made my blue eyes jump out—like Mom used to say, my best feature, even with the extra folds of lid. Susan and I were going to our weekly happy hour at the Drunken Sailor, known to locals as the senior buffet. I waited on my screened porch, feet up, happy my condo was a top-floor end unit. No one walked by me or on top of me—complete privacy.

The combination of the salty breeze ruffling up under my skirt, the view of the inland waterway and the fishing boats returning, and some good jazz playing made this my favorite time of the day. Well, usually my favorite time, but I knew Alyssa's phone call would bring bad news. She rarely called, so whenever I heard "Hello, Mom," I prepared for the worst.

Susan's heavy footsteps resounded along the outside corridor accompanied by her bubbly ex-smoker's voice. "Hey, Maureen, I've been waiting on you. Let's go, I'm starvin'. And you could use a drink, baby."

When we got to the Drunken Sailor, the only seats left in the lounge were two high bar stools. Susan moaned, "Oy, Humpty Dumpty me is supposed to mount that!" So Susan stood at the corner while I perched above her. Her chin barely reached the bar and I felt the urge to pet her curly beige top. At five-foot-five, I was not tall, but I felt like a giant next to four-foot-eleven Susan.

"I'll keep my eyes out for a table," I told her, "but we can just go out for a burger if you're uncomfortable."

"Just order me one of those goldfish-bowl margaritas and I'll snag us some goodies!"

We had the Sailor down to a science. Every week I stayed with our booze and seats while Susan, a buffet pit bull, collected food for both of us. Susan had come of age in Queens and learned her maneuvers from her mother—who could have competed with General Patton. The first time I met Susan's mom she looked me up and down and said, "Sweetheart, doesn't your mother feed you?"

The Sailor's noise had reached a deafening level. Why did these joints play music people had to shout over? But it didn't matter; we were there for the free chow. Sucking on sticky barbecued ribs and inhaling mounds of the spicy lo mein was sybaritic.

Susan took a huge gulp of her drink then grinned up at me. "I hate you, Reenie—I know, *Maureen*. How can you eat all that stuff and stay so thin?"

"'Cause I exercise, sweetie, and I never eat sweets."

"Yeah, why did I ask? I am kinda partial to ice cream and..." Susan shrugged and laughed, causing a ripple visible from her chins down.

When my intake valve forced a pause, I surveyed the room. About half of the fifty or so folks were our generation; the rest were hospital employees from the Sun Medical Center across the street. Nice to see them here instead of on their turf.

My eyes connected with my new neighbor, Bob Goldman. Bob had moved into the next-door condo last month and we'd exchanged a few greetings while riding in the creaky elevator together. He'd told me he was fifty-five, the youngest age allowed at the Gardens. He'd inherited the apartment when his mother died and—the big shocker—he was an RN. I still did not feel comfortable with male RNs poking around my body.

Bob waved and headed over to our corner; I dropped a rib and began cleaning the grease off my hands and face, trying not to remove all my lipstick.

Susan stared up at me, eyebrows arched. "You want I should hold up a mirror so you're *fapitzed* for that handsome and, hmm, young fella?"

"I'm just—shh, here he is." Damn, why was I feeling like a fifteen-year-old virgin?

"Ladies, I see the Gardens are well-represented tonight." Bob's deep voice made me go soft inside, similar to an attack of diarrhea. He was nice-looking, with a Fox News smile and a head of dark wavy hair that spilled over one eye, but his body was what everyone noticed first—he was short and stocky but bursting with muscles. I pictured him figure skating, holding the girl up by one hand on her crotch.

"Susan, this is my new neighbor, Bob Goldman."

Susan shook his hand and said, "So, Bob, you married?"

I gave Susan a shut-it-down look.

Bob laughed. "You are direct. I've been divorced for ten years. Well, I'll tell you my big secret." He held his hand up and grinned. "Don't laugh—that's when I left Wall Street and became an RN."

Susan's mouth dropped open. "*Oy vey.* You were working for Madoff, maybe? Just kiddin'. But a nurse?"

"I could have retired early, even after paying off my ex, but I wanted to do something meaningful with the rest of my life—and it was too late to fulfill my mother's dream—"

Susan sputtered, "You mean every Jewish mother's dream!"

"Yeah. Dr. Goldman."

We all laughed. I was thinking, *Too good to be true, this Goldman.*

"You ladies want to join me later at the Sunset Grill? A great jazz trio is playing there tonight."

Susan immediately declined. I, who had not been alone with any man but the maintenance guy in years, said, "I love jazz—I own every Miles Davis album. But my daughter promised to call me tonight." *Damn. Why didn't I say yes?* I wanted to go but my heart was setting a new arrhythmia record. *He's just a neighbor.*

Bob smiled. "Another jazz lover. I have all the John Coltrane and Miles Davis albums on vinyl—and maybe a hundred others. I still like the sound from my turntable. So, ladies, why don't we all meet here next Tuesday? I'll get out of work early enough to save us a table."

The nanosecond Bob left, Susan started in. "Look at you, your cheeks are blotched with red and you had a goofy smile on your face for this Bob-the-Nurse guy. You've got a crush!" She ha-ha'd in her inimitable croak.

"Ridiculous! He's obviously way too young—even if I wasn't off men for life."

"Yeah, that's why you sucked in your belly and gazed into his eyes like he was the messiah."

We drove home with Susan teasing me until we were both in tears (and a little leakage) from laughing too hard. I did *not* have a crush on Bob. My long-dead sex drive did rev up a little when we rode up or down in the clunking elevator together. And maybe I had timed a few quick exits from the pool when I saw his Porsche pull in. "Oh, hi, Bob. Going up?" *It's hard to lie to yourself.*

As I stepped into my apartment, I remembered the first time John and I stayed there. He'd insisted on carrying me over the threshold, even though we'd been married for over thirty years, and he dumped me right onto the king-size bed. It was a day before the New Year's Eve of Y2K, and we made millennium-love.

"Maureen, my beautiful Irish colleen," he said as he undressed me and pressed all the buttons he knew how to work so well.

I fell asleep imagining being spooned by John's six-foot, two-hundred-pound frame. It was after eleven when I was jolted awake by my talking phone's obnoxious computer voice repeating, "Call from Al-ee-sa."

Damn! She knew I'd already be asleep, but I grabbed the receiver. "Alyssa, hi, hon."

Without even a "hi, how are you," she said, "Mom, I need to come visit for a while. The city's eating me alive." Her voice sounded squeaky, like the Chipmunks, not her usual know-it-all, don't-lecture-me tone.

I knew Alyssa hated Florida. She thought it was just a stepping stone to the graveyard, filled with old, fat bodies that needed to exit more quickly and stop raising the national debt with their hip replacements. But I said what mothers are forced to say—"Of course, come down!"—even though I was thinking, *How long is "a while"?* I loved my daughter, but I saw her so rarely she'd become a stranger to me.

"My plane gets in tomorrow at eleven in the morning. Jet Blue, okay?"

When she hung up, I was still groggy—tomorrow, no notice, what the hell was up? Alyssa had made only one visit to Florida, over a year ago, and had her iPhone in her hand or pocket for the entire visit, constantly tapping out or reading text messages. When we sat down to dinner the first night, the tweety noise signaling a text went off for the hundredth time and she whipped it out and glanced down at the screen. I'd wanted to smash that stupid smartphone.

"Please put that thing away. I feel like you're not even here. It's so rude to…to—"

"I've gotta answer these clients. They never stop calling. Every client thinks they own me."

I reined in my anger, or tried to. "Maybe you need a full-time job, hon. Freelancing sounds too stressful."

"Yeah. I'm looking, but most companies aren't hiring now."

Alyssa never put that damn phone down, but at least she put it on vibrate so I wouldn't hear it. And she disappeared six or seven times a day to suck in nicotine. I'd had a tension headache and a knotted stomach for the entire three-day visit.

Chapter 2

I figured an hour to drive to the Lauderdale airport if I left by 9:30, but Murphy's Law produced a five-lane backup. After an hour of stop-and-go, it finally opened up and the jockeys started zipping along at seventy-five, changing lanes like action movie chase scenes. I stayed timidly in the right lane, occasionally getting stuck in one of those exit-only lanes and panicking while merging left. In my younger days I could navigate New York City traffic like a cabby, but my reflexes were going downhill as my anxiety escalated. Even yoga, my refuge, was no longer relaxing now that I concentrated more on fart-fear than breathing.

The stress of the long delay and my breakfast of granola and coffee were causing an alarming need to get to a bathroom or die of embarrassment. Maybe Susan was right—I ate too much crunchy stuff. Clenching my butt muscles and clenching the steering wheel, I had no brain cells left to contemplate Alyssa's emergency trip. Then my cell rang, and I fumbled through my purse, barely missing a guy cutting me off. I hated answering at sixty miles an hour.

Alyssa's irritated voice crackled in my ear. "Where are you? I'm at Carousel Ten."

Where does she think I am—Hawaii? "Be there in a few minutes—traffic problems."

"Meet you outside at arrivals, okay?"

"No! Inside." Of course I had to park, so I could shit. The clenching was losing power. Poor John often had that problem after his surgery, and the final indignity of needing a diaper destroyed his will to live. At last: airport entrance, short-term parking, me running inside with my jumpy eyes searching for the restroom sign, hoping there would be no line. When I could breathe again, I made it to the baggage claim area and there she was, hauling a huge suitcase off the ramp—the case probably cost an extra hundred to ship.

I tapped her on the shoulder and she jumped as though punched. "Watch this bag. I have another."

No hug, no hello. She whipped around and plunged back into the crowd. Another bag? She used to visit with just a backpack. She returned, towing another mammoth case. "Can you handle that one, Mom?"

"Yes. If I get a hug first."

Alyssa gave me a quick hug like I had leprosy. Her body felt like bones on strings under three layers of T-shirts. Her skin was gray; she looked old. "Honey, I'll leave you at the curb with your monstrosities while I bring the car around."

I hoped the cases would fit in my Prius. Rushing to the parking deck, I trembled with panic. John always said I worried too much, but a mother knows when something awful has happened to her child. While waiting in line to pay the exorbitant parking fee, horror stories about Alyssa ricocheted around my head: she was dying of cancer—no, it must be AIDS—or she was bankrupt. When she lived with Shithead, the artist who'd dumped her out of his apartment last year, she'd needed huge "loans" to get her own digs.

As I pulled up to Arrivals, I watched Alyssa suck in a last drag and grind out her cigarette in the road. She'd told me she gave it up a few months ago, but I zipped it as we sweated the two cases into my car. Before the car started, she said, "I've got a terrible migraine. Sun is killing me," then wrapped a scarf around her eyes like a person ready for the firing squad. Well, conversation didn't mix with me and heavy traffic anyway.

It was 1:30 when we pulled in to the Garden's parking area, then made our way up the walkway. The water aerobics gals were splashing away, gaping at our little parade. In the sunlight Alyssa looked even worse—a bad dye job had left her hair dirty blonde with black roots and her butt had disappeared. Her once cute figure looked like a twelve-year-old boy's. Too old for anorexia, I hoped.

When we entered my apartment, the white leather sofas and pale marble floors were dazzling in the sun. Alyssa cringed.

"How about some lunch, sweetie?" As I said this, I recognized my talk-to-little-children voice and remembered she hated being called "sweetie."

"Mom, ah, no thanks. Need to sleep…talk later."

I heard a flush, then the blinds snapping shut in the guest room, the bed squeaking, then silence.

I was afraid to leave the apartment—maybe she was dying. I sat on my porch with a yogurt smoothie and my laptop, trying to read my email, failing to focus. Migraines did run in my family. My aunt had needed my mother to race over and take her kids whenever she had one. I'd always thought my aunt faked her pain so my mother would babysit her three children—until the day we found Aunt Barb puking all over her living room when we got there to pick up my cousins.

***

Alyssa was an only child. After trying to get pregnant for years, I spent many hours with a fertility specialist and went through a battery of embarrassing tests—my vagina was frequently invaded by bizarre apparatus, often with an audience of technicians. Later, the doctors said it was unlikely I could have children. John and I accepted this. I'd been teaching computer systems at a two-year college and was almost relieved. I loved my work. So I almost fainted when, at age forty-one, I went to my gynecologist thinking I had a disease and learned I was pregnant. John, his family, and my family were all thrilled, toasting with champagne—but I needed a shrink, not a drink. Our life was perfect as it was: I was chair of my department, and John and I traveled, played tennis, and skied. We'd be old by the time *it* hit high school. However, after she was born, I looked down at her pink, Cesarean-perfect face and cried: a jumble of joy and awe, and, probably, excess hormones.

***

Damn, I'd fallen asleep and just missed spilling a smoothie on my computer. Alyssa rattling around in the bathroom had woken me up. The shower ran for at least fifteen minutes. What do people do in the shower for so long? When she finally emerged, I smelled smoke, and my first words were, "You can't smoke in this apartment." Couldn't I have waited? Of course she knew that from her past visit.

"It helps my migraines to have some nicotine. I'll go down the three damn flights next time!"

I ignored her nasty remark. "You want a sandwich or something?"

"No. Just some coffee right now."

I got us both coffee and put a few muffins on a plate since she looked starved, then we sat on the porch. The sun had moved overhead so the light was no longer blinding and there was a cool breeze. "So, you want to tell me why you're here, dragging all four seasons of your clothes?"

"I got evicted...sort of."

"Sort of? Why didn't you call for help?"

"I can't talk about stuff yet." That was followed by a long pause while she stared into space. "I had mono...have mono, and haven't been able to do much work for a few months." She started to choke back sobs. I moved to hug her but she waved me away. "Just need some time to get better, lots of rest, okay?"

I was overwhelmed, but said, "Sure. Stay as long as you need," while thinking: my bridge group meets here, my spirituality group meets here, and there was Bob, maybe a jazz club date with Bob. Stupid thought—mooning over a guy who had never asked me out, while my child was ill. What a selfish mother. I hated myself, but I couldn't help feeling invaded.

"What did your doctor say? Do you need to see my doctor?"

"I'm taking an antidepressant. There's not much anyone can do for mono."

"Food. It looks like you need to eat better. That I can do."

For the first time, she smiled. "Yeah. I've been dreaming about some of your cooking. Can you make the pasta and asparagus dish I love?"

"Sure. Want to come to the market with me?"

"No. I'm still headachy."

"I'll be back soon. Call my cell phone if you need anything, or call Aunt Susan. I know she'll want to see you."

I made it to the market on autopilot. It could have been "Beam me up, Scotty" for all I remembered of driving and parking. I was pushing my cart, unaware of the visual bombardment of cereals, snacks, sodas, and the loud "shopping" music, when a crash brought me back to reality. I'd whacked my cart right into Bob's cart. Damn, would he think I bumped into him on purpose?

"Oh. Bob. I'm sorry. I was in a daze."

"Hey. You did look like you were sleepwalking. What's up?"

"Well, my daughter just arrived from Brooklyn and I…" *Fucking tears. How not to impress a guy.*

"What's wrong? Can I help?"

His warm baritone voice melted some permafrost inside me. "No, no. I don't know. My daughter. She's not well. Says it's mono. Do people in their twenties get mono?"

"Yeah, but it usually goes away with a good rest."

"Thanks, Dr. Goldman." I tried to smile—I'm sure it looked like a crooked grimace.

"Why don't you stop at my apartment for a drink on your way back? And I'll put a Coltrane album on for you."

"Well…yes, great. As soon as I remember how to shop."

He's just a neighbor being neighborly. Don't read too much into this, I told myself. But what if…? What did Susan call women who dated younger men? Cougars, that was it. But he was too young and virile for me—me, who did not want anything to do with the messy business of sex again. A good cuddle, maybe? I laughed and sniffled as I quickly plopped groceries into my cart. I was emotionally exhausted, so it wasn't a good time to visit Bob. And Alyssa was waiting for me.

Chapter 3

When I left the market, I dug through my purse twice before remembering my keys were in my pocket. Then I had to use the unlock button five times to listen for the beeps to locate my car. Lately, I was always losing things—and, worse, losing names of people from my porous brain. How could I spend time with a fifty-five-year-old guy? How long before he noticed my malfunctioning memory, my increased gas production, my crop of skin crinkles—the list kept growing. How absurd.

Clanking up in the dying elevator with my canvas bag of groceries, I decided to walk quickly past Bob's apartment, but he was sitting on his screened porch, not two feet from me. "Hey, Maureen, slow down! I made us some margaritas. I know you like them."

Oh, that voice—the man should be a preacher. Or in his case, a rabbi. "I'm kinda late." I paused. "But I could use a drink." In addition, I could hear the rich sounds of Miles Davis's trumpet filling the air—I'd been in love with his jazz since college. Bob had a pitcher of drinks on the porch, so I asked, "Can we go inside, please? I know

I sound pathetic, but I need privacy from my daughter." I still could not form a proper smile; my lips would not function and I could feel a muscle twitching under my eye.

We settled inside on facing love seats. I could tell the old, overstuffed furniture was his mother's—men and bold floral prints do not mix. We both sipped silently for a couple of minutes—not an uncomfortable silence. *Kind of Blue* enchanted us; I think we both felt the ghost of Miles Davis in the room. I looked around and saw a wedding photo of his mother and father and a few family pictures in heavy silver frames.

"Bob, why didn't I ever see your mother around here?"

"She was in the Memory Care unit at Brookline Home for the last three years—Alzheimer's. It was really a blessing when she died. It was still wrenching for me. At the end, I withheld medication when she got pneumonia." He coughed and turned away. "I knew it was the right thing to do, but..."

"I'm sorry...Did you have any siblings to help you?"

"Ah, families...my brother is too important to leave his law firm. He felt since Mom didn't recognize him anymore, why should he waste any time with her?"

"I went through something similar with my mother—and alone."

We were silent again as Coltrane's "My Favorite Things" replaced Davis.

"Your sound system is wonderful. The band could be in this room." I swayed to the tempo. "Listening to a good trumpet or sax playing is therapy for me—the vibrations bleach out my stress—better than Valium." Oh, great, I sounded like *Valley of the Dolls*. I'd sucked down the tall drink in record time and could feel my nerves relaxing, my muscles turning to soft butter. The eye twitch was gone.

"Then come with me on Saturday night. There's a fantastic trumpeter at the Davis Center, Dominic Derasse. It's a chamber music group, but you'll feel Dominic's sound in your gut. Meet me here at seven?"

Was this an actual date or did he feel sorry for me? The booze gave me the courage to say, "Yes. I'd love to. I haven't been to a live concert in a long time." And I hadn't been on a date in, oh golly, forty-some years!

"Do you play an instrument, Bob?"

"Yeah. My first love. I played upright bass in college. We had a terrific little jazz band...but I haven't played in years." He frowned and sighed. "Let me pour you another drink."

"No. My daughter's waiting for me to feed her and I've been out too long." Now I sighed.

"If there's anything I can do to help you with your daughter, please call me. I know all the ER docs and they know everyone else."

"Thanks." He sounded like an eager boy scout, sincerely wanting to help. "By the way, do you have any children?"

He suddenly looked stricken, as if I'd assaulted him. "That's a long, sad story for another time."

He walked me to the door, his arm hovering around my waist. I shivered. Then I realized I'd left my grocery bag behind the sofa and he ran back for it. Damn, I was ready for memory care.

When I opened my apartment door, Alyssa was stretched out on the sofa staring at her MacBook. She snapped it closed and sat up when I came in.

"Hi, hon. I've got all the stuff for dinner. Ready in half an hour."

"Thanks, Mom."

"You want to help? Maybe chop some garlic—"

"Can't. My migraine med makes me woozy."

"Can you have some wine with all your meds?" Wrong question—again.

"All my meds! It's just two…but you're right, wine and migraines don't mix."

Alone in the kitchen, I put away groceries, filled the pasta pot with water, chopped garlic and asparagus, located the sun-dried tomatoes, all the time asking myself how I ended up with a daughter who was truly a stranger to me. I love conversations with friends, but I'd been tongue-tied with Alyssa since her freshman year of high school—always afraid to say something that would push her further away. Now she obviously had some formidable secret. I felt helpless. I wished John was still alive.

***

Alyssa's childhood had flown by with few difficulties until her freshman year in high school. One lovely fall afternoon, I came home from work early and found her and three friends high in a cloud of fragrant smoke. They didn't even hear the door slam.

I was shocked and screamed, "All of you, get out!" Her friends grabbed their gear and ran. "Alyssa, you're grounded for a month."

"For trying pot? Everybody tries it. I didn't even like it."

Too angry for thought, I said, "I'll find a march-and-pray school for you if anything like this happens again."

From that episode on, Alyssa tested us often. Her curfew became a farce, our advice was ignored, and the sweet smell of marijuana often scented her room. John and I tried grounding her, then no allowance, adding on no friends over, no overnights, but she got worse each month. I learned it's impossible to know what a teenager is doing—without trust, the parent-child relationship becomes worse than the Palestinians versus the Israelis. After a year of crime and punishment, she took a computer animation class and her world blossomed. As a high school junior, she won awards and recognition for her work and even got a small scholarship from Pratt. She was gifted. She knew it and used it.

Her father's involvement also improved her attitude at home. In February of her second year of high school, when her rebellion had reached its peak, I'd retreated from the dining room to avoid yelling at Alyssa again. I heard John say, "I am the luckiest man on earth to have such a beautiful, smart daughter. I want you to come to the construction site with me all next week during school break. Watch how I boss people around!"

I stayed next to the door to hear her answer. "I can't; I've got a term paper due, I—"

John used his construction-boss voice. "Sweetheart, you can and you have no choice."

Alyssa and her dad had always been close, and the week together cemented their relationship. After grousing and making him late the first day, she ended up loving her week with her dad at the work site. I heard about their outdoor lunches together, her special pink hardhat. She drove his truck, laughed with the crew, learned how to measure and hammer, and talked about it every night for weeks.

***

When dinner was almost ready, I called Alyssa to set the table— no answer. She must have gone down for her "medicinal" nicotine. I arranged the food, keeping the pasta warm. A few minutes later she came in enveloped by a miasma of smoke. I was a smoker before Alyssa was born, and the smell made me crave a cigarette. I'd snuck quite a few during John's last months. Would I survive my daughter's recovery?

"Help yourself from the kitchen. And there's goat cheese to put on top of your pasta, a baguette on the table."

"Thanks. It looks beautiful! The colors—tomatoes, asparagus, pasta, parsley—nice."

When she squeezed by me to get to the table, she raised her eyebrows and grinned. "Mom, do I smell booze on your breath? Am I driving you to drink already?"

"Don't know how you can still smell with the cigarettes." Again I wanted to take back my words, so I laughed a little to smooth things over. She had, after all, used humor. "I just ran into a friend and stopped in for a quick drink on the way home."

"Gal-pal or guy?"

She was suddenly talkative—and a bit nosy. "A guy, but just a neighbor—not even a friend, really." I was not about to tell her about my future "date"—that was a discussion I wasn't even ready to have with myself yet.

We were silent for a few minutes as we concentrated on the food. I watched Alyssa carefully. She couldn't sit still—her legs, her arms, even her face, were in constant motion. She kept scratching at various body parts, but I was happy to see that at least she ate heartily.

I sipped my iced tea and asked, "Do you want to talk about 'stuff' yet? I'm very worried about you, and—"

"Really, Mom, I just need to get better, then get a full-time job. And no more freelance—no one ever pays you on time, and it's either overwork or no work." She paused for a drink and a scratch. "And it's too lonely. I can't work alone anymore." She looked like a waif, so thin and pale.

"Are you flat broke? Do you have any savings?"

I saw tears welling up in her eyes as she dug out an old tissue and blew her nose. "I'm down to my last hundred bucks and two maxed-out credit cards." She pushed her plate away. "Fuck, Mom, can't I rest a little before the inquisition? Get a little stronger..."

"Alyssa, for heaven's sake—I'm trying to assess the problem, see where I can help."

"Just...I know...later..."

She took our plates into the kitchen and rinsed them, then told me she was going for a walk. She did not wait for a response, just grabbed her backpack and walked out.

I was definitely *not* going to survive.

I cleaned up and teared up. My two-bedroom apartment was already starting to feel like a broom closet. I'd taken my files, my printer, and some of my books out of the guest room and they were stacked on my closet floor and on top of my dresser. My home was usually House and Garden perfect and I already hated this mess. I thought about what a precocious child Alyssa had been. For her first five years I dropped her at the day care center on my campus so I could visit her between classes. By the time she learned to walk she would shout, "Mama, mama," and waddle over to be picked up whenever I came in. By the time she was three, she would plop onto my lap on breaks and show me all the drawings she'd made—she was already displaying a budding talent.

After she started school, she spent her odd days off in my office and often accompanied me to classes. One day, when she was six, she got to my classroom before me and stood up on a chair. I heard her telling the class, "Listen up and settle down. I want to see your code from yesterday." The class was laughing when I stepped in.

She often imitated me at home too, making John laugh and clap: "My two professors." John had a successful construction company and was probably smarter than I, but he was always a little awed he'd married a college professor. I always told him a community college was no Harvard.

Alyssa grew up so quickly—by middle school she had no time for us, no interest in my college anymore, just busy with friends and computers. Thankfully that was before smartphones and teens overdosing on social media! I insisted we eat dinner together every weeknight or we'd never have seen her. She was never rude, always said please and thank you, but always had homework to do or events to go to. She had no interest in doing anything with us—well, especially me. Normal, according to most "how to parent a teenager" self-help books. Compared to the horror stories in some of these books, we'd been doing okay.

It was getting late—it had been two hours since Alyssa took her "walk." There was little to walk to around the Gardens: about a mile to the beach, a few bars on the main road, and otherwise just residential homes or condos in the immediate area. I was getting frightened, so I called Susan and told her the tale of my agonizing day.

"Don't worry. Alyssa's a smart gal who knows her way around New York. She probably just stopped at a café or she's sitting on the beach."

"At 9:30? Maybe she got lost. Maybe I should drive around and search for her."

"Did you call her cell phone?"

"Of course! It went straight to voice mail."

"If she's not home by eleven, call me back and we'll both go. Okay? And don't forget, I'll see you tomorrow at the Blue Goddess. After your yoga class, which you're going to, I hope."

Should I call the police? And tell them what? "My twenty-seven-year-old might be lost walking around Fort Lauderdale; yes, she's got a cell phone; no, she's not disabled..."

Lying down on the sofa with an herbal mask over my eyes, I dozed off. Voices on the walkway outside my porch door made me jump up so fast I stubbed my big toe on the coffee table. Excruciating pain radiated through my body. I hop-walked to the door, then froze—it was Bob's unmistakable voice harmonizing with Alyssa's laughter. Feeling like Mommy-the-Crone, I waited, listening.

I heard Alyssa say, "Thanks, Bob. I owe you one. I didn't realize how far I'd wandered. And Mom would *really* be pissed if I was any later!"

"Happy I could help. I live right next door if you need anything. Your mom has my number. Good night, now."

When I heard her key in the door, I stepped back and took a deep breath. I needed a Valium—or a gag. As she stepped in, I blurted out, "Alyssa, where the hell have you been? I am too old to worry like this." I tried to keep my voice in a normal range, but I could hear my own fury.

"God, Mom. I've lived in the City for almost nine years. I had my cell with me."

"Your cell is no good if you don't answer it!"

"I had it turned off. So no one could bother me."

"But you're sick. That's why you're here! Sick people with migraines don't go for three-hour walks."

"I found a bar with a good guitarist playing. The weather was perfect, so I sat outside, had a Diet Coke, and listened."

I was almost afraid to ask, but couldn't stop myself. "And how did you end up with Bob?" Did my voice sound like a jealous old fool's?

"He was at the next table with some guys in scrubs. We all started talking. He said he knew you, heard I was visiting, offered me a ride back."

"I almost called the police—I was terrified something happened to you. Next time, answer your damn cell phone or call me."

"Jeez, check in, check out, like high school!"

"You came here to get better!" I sucked in air, lowered my voice. "Listen, I'll be at yoga till about eleven tomorrow. Let's talk after and figure out how this can work—for both of us."

We retreated. I did take a Valium—I saved them for very stressful times and only took a minute dose, but I knew it was the only way I'd sleep.

Chapter 4

I desperately needed my yoga class to regain my equilibrium, so I pushed past my fart-fear and surrendered my mind to the asanas. By the time we were all lying down in the final resting asana, known as corpse pose, I felt cool water washing through my brain thanks to Anika, who gently pulled on my head, then massaged my temples—bliss.

Finally, the class, in unison, intoned the final *Om*, the vibrations of the ancient and holy sound filling the room. Rolling up my mat, I noticed our Lothario, Leo, next to me.

"Nice class today," he said. At first I heard, *Nice ass today.* "You were really into it," he added.

"Yeah. I love this class, but I never saw you here before." I knew I used my puke-it-out voice; I didn't want anything to interfere with my bliss.

"I've been going to a different yoga studio, but I think I'll be coming here from now on. I like Anika's hands-on technique."

Was he being provocative? I thought not—this time. "Anika is the best. She removes all my stress."

"By the way, Maureen, I heard your daughter is visiting. Think I saw her yesterday—well, anyone under fifty does stand out at our Shangri-La!"

"Yup. She's here to rest; she's been ill."

"Don't know if you heard, but I'm a retired internist. If you need any help, please call me." He gave me the traditional bow with his hands in prayer position and said, "*Namaste.*"

"*Namaste,* and thank you." I bowed back. Did my voice show my surprise at how pleasant the encounter was? He didn't sound like an old roué today.

I packed up my yoga stuff and rushed to the Goddess Café to meet Susan. I ignored the Tarot cards on the table and the ads for palm readings, ding-dong therapy, and goddess knows what else, and concentrated on the world's best scones. The place fit well with my yoga afterglow. Susan and I were sitting on the patio, where each table was a private arboretum surrounded by potted palms, the breezes making tree music.

Susan looked me over like I was a banana with defects. "Well, *bubala,* you do look radiant. Maybe I should take up yoga. They have fat-lady yoga?"

"They have beginner yoga. You'd like it. I'd go with you."

"Maybe. I'll think." We both paused to eat our scones, Susan's dripping homemade strawberry jam. I tried to sip my cappuccino without destroying the heart floating on top. Susan, having inhaled scone number one, looked over at me. "So, how are you and Alyssa? I assume she came home last night."

"What a night!" My voice was escalating into soprano range. "She got home about eleven, and guess who drove her home from the local bar?" I paused, and Susan shrugged. "Bob. Dr. Goldman!" Damn, I'd lost all my yogic calm in one outburst. I tried to return to three-part breathing.

"Maureen, hon. Calm down and listen up. You can't fix Alyssa. And you need to give her a long leash. Why don't you invite me to dinner? Maybe I can talk to her."

I remembered how close Susan and Alyssa used to be—Susan never married and she'd spoiled my daughter at every holiday and birthday, at least until Alyssa stopped acknowledging the entire adult population.

"She still calls you Aunt Sue. Come over on Friday." I sat up straight and grinned. Sue noticed my transformation. "Now, for my big news. Ta-da!" I hammered a little rhythm on the table. "I'm going on my first date in forty-three years on Saturday! To hear a trumpeter. And I'm terrified."

"The young Dr. Goldman, I presume!" Susan laughed and wagged her finger at me. "You are now an official cougar."

"I feel like an official idiot. Sixty-nine versus fifty-five. Am I nuts?"

"You look great. You could pass for fifty-five—that's why I hate you."

I smiled, hoping it was true—not the hate part—and replied, "If no one sees my varicose veins or, heaven forbid, my naked pudenda!"

"Well, I hope he doesn't get there any time soon!"

"Of course not! I never want to deal with sex again. It's yucky and—"

"Stop obsessing. Just enjoy the date and the music. He probably goes out with hot young nurses, so don't worry about what'll probably never be on the menu. What's it your yoga gal says? 'Live in the moment.'"

"Thank you, Sue-the-Guru."

"And one more thing to think about. Alyssa is probably still depressed about her father. You told me she never, ever talks about him."

"Oh, boy. I'm on overload today, but you're right. Thanks for always being there for me." I grabbed her hand and gave it a squeeze.

When I got home, it was after eleven. I knocked on Alyssa's door and there was no answer. I peeked into her room—bad mistake. It looked like a sale day at Filene's Basement. Clothes, computer wires, papers, and makeup paraphernalia everywhere. I moved to the guest bathroom and it looked like a trapped bear had floundered around in there. *Oh, we need to talk.*

How did she end up with so many problems? Smart, talented, and pretty, and she was never a latchkey kid. I usually got home from work before she finished school, and I thought I was a decent mom. Had I loved my career too much? Maybe.

However, Susan may have pointed out the biggie—Alyssa never wanted to talk about her dad's death. She'd avoided us during the years when her father looked sickly. Of course, she was in college and then became an instant success—and permanently overworked. Toward the end, when John was wheelchair-bound, I'd called Alyssa.

"Your dad wants to see you. He doesn't have too much longer and he wants to have some time with you before he's too medicated to talk. Can you spend next weekend here?"

"I'll try, but I have two clients breathing down my neck—as soon as I'm finished I'll be there."

"Can't you tell your clients the situation?"

"They don't give a shit." She paused. "Gotta tell Dad—one of my jobs is for Pixar. Through an agency, but I still might have to go to California soon. Put him on and I'll tell him about it."

John was thrilled to hear about her Pixar job and it perked him up until he realized he might never see her again. I hated Alyssa then, and had probably never forgiven her for not visiting her dying father more. Had I not recognized she'd dealt with his illness by pretending it wasn't happening? Maybe Susan was right and Alyssa was suffering a delayed reaction to loss.

***

At noon Alyssa came in dragging a huge laundry bag. She looked exhausted. I told her to put her extra clothes into my storage locker on the first floor.

"Can we sit down now and talk without yelling?"

She sank onto the sofa with a groan.

"Now, tell me what's happening. What do you need?"

"I hate to ask, again, but I do need money—and I'll pay you back, I promise!"

How many times had I heard that promise? But I held my tongue.

Her eyes looked everywhere but avoided looking at me. "I have to get to my doctor in New York once a month. I think I can fly in, see her, and fly back the same day."

Once a month! How the hell long is this visit to be? "Alyssa, that's three hundred just for the flight! Can't we find you a local doctor?"

"Well, at least for this month, I've gotta go back—she's a psychiatrist and it's hard to change quickly. If you could loan me two thousand, I won't have to ask every time I need cigarettes or meds."

My head was reeling. Over the past three years she had "borrowed" more and more money—she'd always had a convincing reason, and I was always involved with John's illness and then my sad escape to Florida. "Okay. But why a shrink?"

"It's hard to talk about everything yet." She paused and drank some juice. From her voice I knew the tears were building up again. "I might be a little bipolar—"

"Then wouldn't your antidepressant be bad for that?" *Like I knew.*

"I'm on a few meds. Didn't want to worry you." She hesitated. "One is sort of...experimental."

I felt run over by a garbage truck. I did not want to deal with her problems. My face must have reflected my pain. She almost shrieked,

"Mom, as soon as I feel good enough to work, I'll get back to the City, or out of here at least!"

"Don't worry. We'll work it out. And getting better is your work now." I got up and gave her a hug—this time she didn't push me away.

I debated asking her how she was dealing with her dad's death—I didn't want to push her away again. Finally I said, "One more thing, Al. I hope you're able to talk about your father's death with your shrink. I feel guilty I couldn't—"

"Don't! Stop! We've talked about it…a little."

I called Susan later and told her some of Alyssa's woes and about my alternating between anxiety about her health and dread about her need to stay indefinitely. "Can you get the Board to allow her a long stay?"

"No problem. But I can't believe she's bipolar. At dinner tomorrow, give me some time alone with Alyssa—get stuck cooking or unclogging a toilet."

"Well, keep that to yourself unless she opens up."

"What! You think I'm a *yenta*? Calm down. And let me do the talking at the Board meeting on Saturday. They all owe me a favor or two."

Susan had been on the Board for a year, and she'd turned the complex around financially—services were better (except my elevator) and we were the first complex to have our condo fee go down. She'd had her own accounting firm in lower Manhattan for over twenty years. I was still surprised she decided to move to

Florida. In New York, Susan always said, "When you go over a bridge or through a tunnel you've left all culture behind." She did tell me a few months ago, "Fort Lauderdale is okay—it's got a few Jews, a little culture, and much better weather than the City."

"Before you hang up, I forgot to tell you what a nice conversation I had with Leo at yoga the other day. I'm going to stop assuming he's only a seventy-something-year-old sex addict."

"Then maybe he'll be an ally for us on the Board. Just relax."

***

Thursday dinner was quiet. I brought in Chinese food: spring rolls, orange beef, fried noodles, and veggies. Alyssa's slight sunburn gave her a healthier look and she was eating well. I still noticed her twitchiness, though. She tried to keep her hands on her legs to quiet all her limbs. I'd read somewhere that psychotropic drugs cause tics—maybe that was the problem.

Conversational platitudes ruled the evening from Alyssa. "Great spring rolls." "What's for dessert?" And a bit later, "Really tired—haven't exercised in ages."

She was headed to her room with her appendage, the laptop, choosing to download movies and watch them alone rather than joining me for TV in the living room. "I'm in the middle of a series and I want to finish off the season."

"Alyssa, wait. I checked with my Schwab account and I'll need all your checking account info to wire money—and the name and address of your bank too."

"My account is in my corporate name, Animate-it, Inc. I'll give you a blank check to use." She started walking away, then turned back. "And thanks, Mom." A half-smile twitched her lips and I actually got a quick hug, initiated by my daughter! Wow. Of course, the two-grand loan probably inspired it. With a trip to NYC, meds, and probably more than seventy dollars a week just for cigarettes, it wouldn't last long.

I turned on my TV and examined every show available, moving the guide up and down, then looked at programs I'd saved on my DVR: *Desperate Housewives* (I was a closet addict), *Parenthood* (too sweet for this parent tonight), and twenty-five episodes of *Golden Girls* I saved for quick pick-ups. Nothing appealed to me. My monkey mind was flying from limb to limb in a jungle of worries. Tomorrow Susan was coming to dinner, but I really needed to get Alyssa out of the apartment while I got ready for my big date the next night. I was not ready for a mother-daughter discussion about Bob.

I called Susan—she must surely have been sick of my whining. "Hey, girlfriend. I need another favor. Can you take Alyssa somewhere for the evening on Saturday?"

"You want I should clear the way for Dr. Goldman prepping?"

"Well…yes. I just want some privacy from Alyssa—it could be awkward."

"There's an improv group at the college. I'll get her to go."

I breathed a sigh of relief. "Thank you, dear."

"And let's cancel tomorrow's dinner. Two nights in a row might be too much of Aunt Sue."

"Okay. And I'll see you at the Board meeting."

Chapter 5

At 8:00 a.m. on Friday morning I was gasping in pain at my core class. My sadistic trainer loved to combine weights with movement and we were doing forward lunges with full curls. Maybe using ten-pound weights was a little optimistic, but I refused to stop and pick up lighter ones. The tiny woman next to me, Pam, who was over seventy and did not have a fat cell left, spent her life at the gym—seven days a week. She was hoisting fifteen-pound weights, but could not hold her form. The teacher constantly berated her for lifting more than she was able—she was more fanatical than I.

Pumping iron was an obsession with me—it strengthens bones. My mother's fragile bones had made her last years hell. Compression fractures of her spine caused her incessant pain and hunched her over her walker like a letter C. I would hear her trying to get up off the toilet, saying, "Shit-shit-shit-get-up-shit." An appropriate curse for the bathroom.

"Mom, do you want some help?" I often asked, although I hated helping her off the john. The sight of my mother's old naked body always repulsed me.

"No, shit-Icandoit-shit."

Until her last month on earth she almost always made it to and from the toilet alone—sheer willpower—her walker whacking into walls and furniture. Even when they had alarms attached to her bed and wheelchair, she ignored the ear-splitting beeps and went her way. I'd vowed to take pills and check out before I needed alarms attached to me.

My mother died a month after John. I had them both cremated—John and I had decided we would not take up land in a cemetery. I ended up with two brown boxes of ashes staring at me from the bureau in my bedroom. Alyssa refused to join me when I spread John's ashes over his beloved perennial garden. (I hoped John's Asian lilies were still rising.) I had a Unitarian Universalist service for John in the lovely white church in Summit, New Jersey. A few friends were shocked to learn I had no service for my mother, but I was in too much pain to plan another funeral.

***

On Saturday, my big-date day, I woke up stiff and creaky from too many push-ups and popped a couple of Aleve. Alyssa was still asleep—she and her computer had stayed up late together the past two nights. I had not told her about the Board meeting. I put on some extra makeup and a cute pair of white capris with a low-cut blue and white top. Most of the Board members were old geezers so it couldn't hurt.

At eleven I went down to the clubhouse and took a seat next to Susan at the big table. Leo sat across from me and gave me a smile and his usual wink. Susan kicked me under the table—reminding me of our college days together—and I struggled to suppress a giggle as I kicked her back.

The Board president, William, looked like an Old Testament prophet with his intense yellow eyes. His deep Georgia-accented voice said, "Let's all get goin'. Y'all have the agenda. I put Maureen on first." He looked over at me.

Susan spoke up for me, telling the Board my lovely daughter just needed to stay with me to recuperate from her illness. The result was Alyssa could stay for a month, then I had to check back with the Board. The thought of more than a month with Alyssa made me grit my teeth.

I slipped out the door and went off to get a mani-pedi. I'd only had five manicures in my life before moving south, but pedicures during Florida's long sandal season were de rigueur—especially for aging feet. Bright fuchsia nails take the eyes away from spider veins, just like the right necklace diverts the eyes from the beginnings of chicken-neck. My neck wasn't too bad yet—*if* I maintained my posture—but short of a facelift, neck lift, and eyelid lift, camouflage was required. Especially for wannabe cougars.

I had no illusions about my "date." Susan was right—a fifty-five-year-old ER guy surely dated hotties from the hospital, and he had money, or said he did. I supposed that not many younger women liked jazz or chamber music—they probably listened to some romantic drivel.

Did I want or expect anything other than a friendship with Bob? No—and not for sex, for sure. I couldn't even watch all the disgusting sex they put in modern movies. Why did they need to show sweaty, naked bodies, banging away and moaning? And why, my enquiring mind wanted to know, did the women on *Sex and the City* always wear push-up bras while naked and fucking? I knew the little machine in my nightstand hadn't been used in a couple of years—probably the batteries were as dead as I was.

The lovely Thai immigrant, Parichat, gave an incredibly sensual pedicure—I went to her once a month. After a hot soak in a vibrating foot-tub, she scrubbed up to your knees with lavender-scented oatmeal, then massaged cream from your toes up your calf. I always moaned a few times—maybe my erogenous zones had migrated down to my feet. Gravity.

I left Parichat, feeling renewed, and grabbed a Vietnamese crepe for lunch—Alyssa could manage without me. I got home about two and saw Alyssa at the pool. I helloed and waved but she didn't see me. Leo, however, gave me another little yoga bow—hmm.

I plopped down on the porch with my laptop to check email. Alyssa came in from her hangout, the pool.

"What time are you meeting Susan tonight?" I asked.

"At six. Aunt Sue acted like no one else on earth would go with her. Why aren't you going?"

"Oh, I'm going to a boring chamber music concert tonight."

After I heard "Goodbye, Mom," I gagged down an egg on toast. Did the invitation include dinner? I didn't think so and was too embarrassed to call him and ask. Then I got down to work.

It was my Junior Prom night all over again. I tried on and rejected two skirts and three pairs of slacks, finally deciding on my skinny white "dress" jeans. They made my butt look like Jennifer Aniston's—yoga does work. After considering three T-shirts, I chose a black silk shell topped by a hand-painted scarf. I kept fussing with my hair, almost frying it with the curling iron. My eye makeup made me look like a raccoon, so I washed it all off and started over. I would never be satisfied with my sixty-nine-year-old looks. I'd been considered pretty my whole life, but the last five years had been painful to watch as the deeper crevices accented my mouth. I was ready to call off the date. Butterflies danced in my stomach as though *I* were going on stage. A headache was threatening to join in.

John's old adage popped into my brain: "What is, is." Even as he faced the pain of bone cancer and imminent death, he'd say, "What is, is, sweetheart." *Oh, don't go there tonight.*

At 6:50 I practiced my deep breathing with a short meditation, repeating out loud, "I breathe in peace; I breathe out and smile." When I opened my door, I was surprised to see that Bob was already standing outside my porch.

"Hi. You look great, Maureen."

Breathe out and smile. As we headed for the elevator, I said, "Thanks." He looked terrific—expensive leather loafers, finely-draped pants. All the old farts wore sneakers and wrinkled khakis to everything. I told him, "I've been looking forward to hearing Derasse. I Googled him—he's quite famous—and I listened a little online. Did you know he's with the New Jersey Symphony?" Couldn't I just shut up? Filling uncomfortable moments with words was my trademark.

"Happy to hear you're wired."

Did he think I was too old to use Google? As the elevator rattled down, I told him I taught computer everything at a two-year college for twenty-five years. "But I've been falling behind ever since I retired." *Why did I add that?*

He led me over to his awesome car, the black Porsche I'd been watching for a couple of weeks, and he even opened the door for me. I snuggled into the warm, golden leather.

His car started with a loud, vibrating *vroom*. "A college prof, huh. Pretty impressive, Maureen."

"Not really. I feel like a dinosaur already. I tried Facebook and hated it—I had people I couldn't stand in real life asking to be my friend, and then getting annoyed because I didn't 'friend' them or 'like' them or whatever." As we rocketed down a short stretch of highway, I thought, *Shut up, Maureen—dinosaur—remind him again how ancient you are!*

After he maneuvered like James Bond around some slow traffic, he answered, "I'm too private for Facebook and I find the entire thing juvenile. You'll never find me smiling out of it." He accelerated so my body was glued to the seat back. The roller coaster ride was relieving my anxiety about the date: now I was afraid of dying.

He chuckled. "Two of the docs I work with are on Match.com and they meet women by the dozens."

"And you?" I asked. Why was he mentioning Match.com? Did he want a few dozen? I was going to Google Mr. Goldman as soon as I got home.

"No, not me! I guess it makes sense to advertise when you're available, but I'm still in divorce-doldrums and I love, really love, working in the ER. I work overtime whenever I can."

"Tell me about the ER—it's terrifying to a squeamish person like me."

"Well, when they bring in a trauma case, like a bad car accident or a shooting victim, and the team goes to work with every second counting, it's an adrenaline rush. And I'm good at it." He smiled, and I pictured every medical show I'd ever seen—most gory scenes watched with my hand over my eyes. *From Wall Street to ER. He's too good to be true.*

"I've gotta tell you, though, the most exciting two months of my life I spent in Haiti after the earthquake with a medical team. We were saving lives every minute of every day, and we worked until we passed out."

We pulled into a parking place, which ended conversation for a while as we hustled into the Center and into our seats, fifth row, center—perfect. Two minutes later two violinists and a cellist came out to applause, followed by big, bald Derasse, who got an exuberant welcome. He walked in like a king.

I had no time to read the program as Derasse's powerful trumpet notes captured me—I felt like a cartoon figure floating on the sound waves. Between movements of something Bach, Bob and I just smiled at each other and mouthed, "Wow."

At intermission, we slowly made our way outside into the newly-darkened evening, velvety Florida air enveloping us. People make fun of our humidity, but on nights like this it caresses you.

"He's great—I'm in love," I blurted out. I hoped he realized I meant Derasse.

"I figured you'd be blown away."

We reached a bench and sat down by a tall fountain and listened in silence to the splashing water cascading down three tiers, a little mist cooling us. Bob's arm moved to the back of our seat, just grazing my shoulder. My breath quickened as I felt that long-lost tingle between my legs. Boy, was I easy or frustrated or crazy? I shivered and crossed my legs, leaning away from Bob.

"Are you cold, Maureen?"

"No, but it must be time to get back."

We started back toward the entrance, Bob's hand on my waist as he guided me up the winding path. Oh, yes, that pulse was slyly signaling, scaring me, surprising me; it had been too long, and Bob was too young, and it was too soon. I tripped in my fancy sandals and Bob's arm pulled me a little closer—intoxicating. I swayed.

"You okay, Maureen?"

"Sorry. A bit dizzy. Not dizzy, just...I don't know." I laughed nervously. "I can't tell you how much I enjoy listening to Derasse." A switch to safer conversation, I hoped.

"I have a surprise for you. After the performance, I'll introduce you to Dominic. I knew him when I lived in New York. Haven't seen him in a few years."

I was trying to relax, to shake off my absurd sexual awakening. As we wriggled around people standing in the aisle, over knees and purses and back to our seats, I regained my composure. Derasse marched out with just a pianist. At the end of the first movement, we each turned toward the other, bumping foreheads. My stomach, my nemesis in distress, was spewing out acid at a painful rate and my colon was starting a symphony of growls; farts could not be far off. I shifted uncomfortably and held my breath. When the next movement ended I slipped a Tums from my purse and tried to chew it without making crunching sounds.

At the end, Derasse got a standing O while many "Bravos" rang out.

Bob leaned over and whispered, "It doesn't get much better than this."

"Amen." I was smiling so wide it hurt. "I can't remember when I've been so overwhelmed by sound." Was it the sound? Would it have felt the same with Susan by my side? What was happening to me—the sensible, logical, computer professor—was a fantasy.

We made our way to the aisle and Bob took my hand and led me against the people-traffic, back toward the stage, then through a side door. There was regal Dominic cleaning his trumpet. I barely remembered what he said, what I said, what Bob said. I was drunk without drink.

When we stepped back outside, it was cool for Florida in April. I pulled my sweater tighter. Bob casually slung his arm over my shoulder. "Chilly night," he said.

"Feels good though." *In more ways than one,* I thought. I'd had more touching in one night than in the past few years—the power of touch, the human desire just for a hand to hold, threatened to undo me. My yoga teacher, my pedicurist, my reflexologist, they all gave me some of the touching I craved. *Breathe in peace; breathe out and relax.* Tucked back into the coddling leather, we inched out of the parking lot.

"I've got an early shift tomorrow or we could stop at a great jazz club I know. Maybe next time?"

Did he ask—next time? It was a question? What did it mean? Why did he want to be with me? I answered him with, "Sure, whenever."

Bob put in a CD and sounds of a jazz trumpeter filled the car. I leaned back, listening, thankful to be silenced.

When we got back to the Gardens, the car and the music switched off and I suddenly felt abandoned. I attempted to jump out—a feat not easily done gracefully from a low Porsche with a heavy door.

"I was going to help you out, Maureen."

"Oops. Well, I'm not used to anyone opening doors for me."

We reached the elevator and it started grinding upward. I stared straight ahead, wordless for a change. I was unprepared when Bob leaned over and kissed me on the lips, very softly, no hands, no probing tongue. I stopped breathing and felt faint for the second time that night. The messenger from my crotch was sending alarming signals. I counteracted by thinking, *Maybe I'm just conveniently located next door for future quickies.* As the elevator opened, I jumped away and started to trot toward my door.

Bob caught up and grabbed my hand. "I really like being with you, Maureen. You understand a good silence…and good music."

As we approached my door, I retrieved my hand and fumbled in my purse, finally finding and putting key to lock. "Thank you. I enjoyed the concert. Good night." I didn't look back as I opened the door, just sighed, ready to collapse.

As I stepped inside, I smelled her before I saw her sitting in my lounge chair—putting out her cigarette in a coffee cup. We just stared at each other for a long moment until she said, "Sorry about the upstairs smoke, but a real creepy guy's been hanging around by the designated area tonight."

"Couldn't you get some nicotine gum—the stink stays in my cushions—and it might help you get off them too."

"Won't happen again." After a pause, she asked, "Did you just get back from a date?" She sing-songed the word date. "With that male nurse?" She drew out the word nurse. Her eyes were bugging out.

"Not a real date—just went to hear classical music we both like. Nothing else. I hardly know him." I needed to shut up—drop it. I actually felt tears forming in my eyes; I was glad it was dim on the porch.

"He's kinda young—for you—don't you think?"

"Young for what? Going to a concert together?" I knew I sounded pissed off. *Pull yourself together, Maureen.*

"It just looked *romantical* from here—I thought you two were gonna clench!"

"Don't be ridiculous, Alyssa!" I quickly said good night and ran to my room.

Chapter 6

On Sunday I woke up to pouring rain and howling wind but decided to brave the weather to go to my Unitarian Universalist church. I needed the support of my fellow UUs. Before John and I bought our condo, I made sure there was a vibrant UU congregation in the area—a liberal from the Northeast needs a place in the South to discuss politics and religion without finding crosses burning on her lawn or being verbally attacked.

At the Fort Lauderdale library a year after Obama was elected, an old codger was loudly telling a table of his cronies, "No one will admit to voting for that Kenyan!" Bald heads nodded in agreement as I waded in with, "I voted for him." The spokesman then told his buddies, "Throw her out of the library!" Only one man timidly stood up for my right to be there.

I'd had some interesting remarks from Floridians on my religious affiliation. "You're a what?" said in loud tones. "A UU?"

I try to explain, but most Christians are flummoxed—a "religion" that promises no salvation and has no dogma? "To each his own," is a frequent response, said in demeaning tones. I was raised a strict, Irish-version Roman Catholic. Lots of us "recovering Catholics" have joined UU churches.

My head that Sunday was so full of Bob-thoughts and Alyssa's derision about my date that the sermon on growing anti-Semitism was lost on me. The service ended with all standing, linking arms, and singing "We Shall Overcome." I was reminded of my college days when Susan and I marched for equal rights in every protest in the New York City area. When Medgar Evers was assassinated, we attended several services together around the city. Our social activism cemented our friendship for life.

The singing and the social hour afterwards revived me. I made it home at noon with a sack of groceries. I was putting things away when Alyssa appeared in the entry and asked, her taunting tone raising my hackles, "So, Mom. You're sure you're not dating Nurse Bob?"

"I told you—I hardly know him. We both like the same music, and he happens to live next door."

She gloated over her next words: "Well, ah, there's a message on your phone from him. How old is Nurse Bob, anyway?"

"Please stop calling him Nurse Bob. He's fifty-five and there's nothing going on!" I was breathing hard and could feel the red blotches forming on my face.

"Well, don't get all huffy and have a stroke."

My head was hiding out in the refrigerator, rearranging food, popping out anything growing new life forms. To change the subject, I shouted into the cold storage, "You want lunch?"

"I'm out of here. Meeting Aunt Sue. We're catching an animation show at the college."

As soon as she left I raced to the phone. After the beeps, I heard his too-sexy voice: "Hi, Maureen. Had a great time last night. A Cuban jazz group will be at Club Metronome on Sunday night. We can get a light dinner there. Can you meet me at six at my apartment? I make a mean mojito that'll get us in the mood. Oh, and those Cuban gals really dress, so wear something wild...just kidding."

Oh, boy. That did sound like a real date. I wished Alyssa hadn't heard the message. What should I make of it? And what does a sixty-nine-year-old widow own that's "wild"? Exactly nothing.

Logic—my strong suit—was battling with the emotional mush in my brain. I started making mental lists: *he's too young, duh; he'll break your heart; don't go out with him again; escape while your dignity's intact.* On the other side: *my yoga teacher says live in the moment.* And my yards of skin all yearned for touch. Maybe I should have just found a good massage therapist—naked with hot oils, hot rocks, and hot hands covering most of the territory.

Guilt pushed Bob out of my head. There I was ignoring my daughter and selfishly focusing on my reincarnated teenage emotions. Why hadn't I found some interesting things Alyssa and I could enjoy together? Why hadn't we gone to the beach? Our best family times had been our annual summer vacations at the Jersey Shore. The three of us loved the beach, at least until she turned thirteen and would not go with us unless we brought one of her friends along. We did that only once, because neither child spoke to us or wanted to do anything with us. Family beach vacations had died.

The shock of Alyssa's sudden arrival five days ago had killed off all logical thought, and logic had been my forte. And I was still reeling from her revelations and my suspicion she hadn't yet told me everything. Needing to clear the chatter from my head, I changed and went down to the Garden's water aerobics class, something I rarely did.

While standing in four feet of water with four other women, waiting for the teacher to shout out our orders, I felt a sudden splash cool the back of my neck. I turned and saw Leo had joined the class—here plus the three times in yoga. Was I being stalked, courted, or was it just coincidence?

He smiled and said, "Hi. Perfect day for pool exercise."

I couldn't stop my eyes from glancing down to his bathing suit— he often wore an ill-advised little Speedo. Thankfully, no soft belly was exposed.

I turned away as we all started kicking forward, and then jogging around in the water. One of the women had boobs like speckled beach balls, bobbing up and down with each jog, threatening an escape. She'd never sink with those built-in buoys. Leo had to be enjoying the show.

When we all slogged out of the pool to our towels and chairs, Leo put on a shirt and came to sit next to me. He chug-a-lugged a bottle of water, then cleared his throat. "That was my first time. Fun, huh?" He paused, but I didn't respond. "Never thought I'd find myself in water aerobics, but it's a good workout for my old joints."

He poured the rest of the water down his throat, and continued with no encouragement. "Yoga's my favorite exercise, though; well, it's more than just exercise, isn't it?"

He was trying so hard I had to answer. "Yeah. For me it clears chatter out of my brain—it's the closest I get to meditation."

"Can I drive you to yoga class tomorrow?"

"No, thanks. I'm meeting Susan right after." *Would I have accepted otherwise? Hmm.*

"By the way, how's your daughter doing? Us old docs like to help."

Did I want to share with Leo? He did seem eager, and he was a physician. "Well." I paused. It couldn't hurt to get input from someone who was not emotionally involved, so I plunged in. "She's moody and irritable, for starters. Also, she's jerky and twitchy whenever she's trying to sit still." I shrugged. "Maybe I shouldn't have shared that."

"Everything is part of a diagnosis; go on."

"She has no energy—she hides out in her room watching old TV shows on her computer. She told me she's been diagnosed as bipolar or depressed or both—in addition to the mono. We'll probably drive each other crazy living together in my apartment. That wasn't 'medical,' was it?"

Leo folded his arms and pursed his lips. I didn't like the look he was giving me—I'd seen bad medical news delivered before.

"What!" I asked in a squeaky voice.

"Well. Any group of symptoms could indicate any number of problems. Bipolar plus mono could lead to all the things you mentioned."

"I know there's a 'but' in there. What are you thinking?"

"This involves a confession and has to remain between us. Okay?"

I nodded.

"My son is a physician and he became addicted to Oxycontin a few years ago. Apparently lots of MDs have succumbed to these artificial opiates. He spent some time with me during his recovery. I think it's possible your daughter is recovering from an addiction."

I felt the blood drain from my head, leaving me dizzy. "Oh, no. I can't believe..." There was a kettledrum booming in my brain.

"I'm sorry. It could be all the other things. I'm just trying to help, truly."

I scrambled up and stuffed my towels into a sack, trying to slip my feet into my sandals without falling. "Gotta run. And, ah, thanks. Bye."

As I staggered off with half-on sandals, he said, "Call me if you need to talk or you need help."

As the elevator clunked upward, I thought, *What does an old retired doctor know about addiction?* I tried to put some rough scenes of crack houses from *The Wire* out of my mind. That was the Baltimore ghetto, not professional New York. When I was showered and dressed I went online and Googled "opiate addiction and recovery"—millions of websites! After glancing through a few I knew Leo might be right. Tremors, twitching, mood swings, irritability, restlessness, bankruptcy, loans, loss of job, loss of housing and friends—the symptoms all fit Alyssa.

Then what? Raid her room? Try to find "evidence"? Ask her? Relationship enders, all. Not that we'd had much of a relationship the past several years. Whenever I closely examined my life, I realized my career was my first love, John a close second, and Alyssa, well, I always wanted the best for her, but I knew I never had the momma-bear connection most mothers talk about. John's illness had drained my emotional well for six years, and my precipitous move to Florida had separated us even more. Our communication had been mostly emails for a long time—I could never reach her on the phone. I was sure she always sent my calls to voice mail.

I sat down and totaled up all the "loans" over the past three years, searching through two bank accounts and my Schwab account. Shit. It was over twenty thousand dollars. I hadn't realized. Her reasons for needing money ranged from "broke up with the bastard and need a new apartment" to "have to pay two people who worked for me and my client's a slow payer." Each sounded legitimate at the time.

One of the websites I read said addicts often steal from loved ones. Then I suddenly remembered she'd borrowed my good pearls and ruby ring last year to go to a political dinner. In addition, I was missing the eighteen karat gold medallion I'd inherited from my grandmother. I'd assumed I lost it in the move. Could she have taken it? I'd have a long talk with Susan tomorrow. Maybe she'd noticed something during their two outings.

I took a Valium and lay down with some soft jazz playing, hoping to put worry about Alyssa away.

Chapter 7

Alyssa came back around five. I had fallen asleep on the sofa and was a bit dazed, both from the nap and the Valium. I slurred out, "Hi. Have a good time with Sue?"

"Yeah. An interesting program at the Art Institute. Hope you didn't make dinner. Think I've got food poisoning or something. Gonna lie down."

"Can we talk later?"

"Okay. Oh, by the way, Aunt Sue treated me to some nicotine gum. Workin' on cutting down."

It was after eight when she reappeared from her room and headed straight for the door. Looking back at me, she said, "Back in a few." Slam.

I sat out on my porch. It was a perfect Florida evening, a cooling breeze coming off the ocean and, even though the beach was a mile away, I could hear the waves crashing. Must be a big storm out at sea. Smoky Alyssa came back and was about to walk right by me.

"Alyssa. Sit down! We have to talk. I'm getting more and more worried about you."

She flopped down but said nothing.

I dove in. "Do you realize how antsy and jumpy you are all the time?"

She inhaled deeply, her eyes trying to escape mine, and answered, "Don't worry. It's the lithium. Takes a while to get the dose right. I'll see my shrink on Friday. Maybe she'll change my dose or—"

"Now it's lithium, not an antidepressant. Are you sure that's all—that's the whole problem?" I must have looked as skeptical as I felt because I saw her body stiffen and she gave me a withering look.

"It's not the *whole* problem." Her voice sounded like it was coming from a bullhorn. My screened porch was open to the outside corridor and embarrassment swamped me at the thought of neighbors, especially Bob, listening.

"The mono destroyed my health, made me screw up two important jobs; I lost my apartment and lost friends while I couch-surfed for a couple of months. My career is fucked! And I'm stuck living with a mother who never wanted me." She started to sob, long, choking sobs.

A bomb exploded inside my brain. I finally croaked out, "Alyssa! Of course I wanted you. That's just your depression talking. I'm really hurt!"

Between sobs she said, "I am trying, Mom. Give me some time."

I would have gotten up and hugged her but the way her body was twisted away from me into the big lounge chair, I knew I was not wanted. "I love you, hon. I just don't know what to do."

We were already both drained and I felt useless. I touched her shoulder as I said good night. I'd hide away in my room and watch movies on my laptop.

***

The next morning I arrived at my yoga class and found a spot to hide in the back, not my usual front row. I wasn't sure I could even do a down-dog without passing out. Sleep had eluded me—my mind jumped from thoughts of Alyssa overdosing on some drug in a filthy apartment after paying some gangrenous dealer with a blow job (a scene from an awful movie), to Bob and me dancing a sexy rumba, me dressed in a low-cut, ruffly dress, with a push-up bra. My inner voice was a drunken monkey with ADHD. Thankfully, Anika turned on her slow Indian music and we started class with some easy stretches. Somehow I got through the ninety minutes without falling over, although Anika had to correct my form a few times and my shadow, Leo, turned around to watch me when he could.

I slipped out of class quickly, avoiding Leo, and made it to the Goddess where Susan was waiting at our usual table. She looked me over and said, "You look terrible, *bubala*! You eating enough?"

"No sleep," I gasped. "Don't know where to start."

"Well, I've been dying of curiosity—start with your cougar-date?"

"It made me feel like an old fool. I like him—he's charming and he's a *mensch*, at least he says he is: volunteered in Haiti, loves saving lives in the ER, loves jazz and chamber music, he's almost handsome, and very fit. So why does he want to be with me? Doesn't that make *him* the weird one?

"You're asking me—about romance! My last date was before computers. So just relax and go with the flow, as they say. Just be careful!" Susan used her harsh Queens voice for the last advice.

"Careful of what?"

"Keep your emotions in check. And if you, well, do *it*, make sure he uses a—"

"Stop! I am not going to do *it* with anyone! And, Susan, we're grownups. Call it sex, fucking, intercourse, *shtupping*, but not *it*."

We were laughing and the two women at the next table were leaning towards us, glued to our conversation. I sobered up quickly and lowered my voice as I moved into Alyssa territory. "Sue, what do you think is up with Alyssa? Has she shared her problems with you at all?"

"She hasn't said much, but she's hurting. She avoided any conversation about her health except to say she'll cut down on smoking. Listen, I watched her smoke a few times while we were out. She drags in like it's her last cig before the firing squad; sucks it right down to the filter—the worst kind of smoking. Oh, and she's a little concerned about you dating 'Nurse Bob,' but I told her it was good for you to finally get out."

We were both lost in thought and quietly sipped our lattes until I told her I needed to get home to sleep off last night's explosion with Alyssa. Why couldn't I bring up my suspicion about addiction? It was too painful to fully contemplate—the word *addict* conjured up such frightful images. Bipolar was bad enough.

***

Apparently Alyssa had caught a nasty bug—she barfed up her guts all day Monday and just staggered in and out of the kitchen to get water, Pepto, or Imodium. Meetings and a hair appointment kept me busy most of Tuesday and I needed to stay away from Alyssa's virulent illness. When I'd passed Bob in the parking area and told him I was concerned about Alyssa's glued-to-the-toilet sick, he told me not to worry, a bad stomach flu was going around our complex. "It happens every year about this time. Just keep her hydrated."

Susan called at four to ask when I was picking her up—I had forgotten our weekly date at the Drunken Sailor. I told Alyssa I'd be gone for a couple of hours and she moaned, "I'm not moving, just go."

We got to the Sailor a little earlier, hoping to avoid bar stools, when Susan remembered Bob had promised last week to save us a table. Last week seemed like months ago; I was living in an altered reality! As I scanned the joint, I saw him sitting at a table but—damn!—with an attractive forty-something blond staring up at him. She must have been six feet tall and looked like a model.

I frowned and hooked a finger in their direction. "Let's not bother Bob."

"We should go say hi. Maybe she just sat herself down and he's waitin' for us."

Shit. I had no idea what to do and stood in the entry like a dolt. Then Bob looked right at me and waved us over. No choice. I felt my face filling with blood and my stomach lurching. Maybe I'd caught Alyssa's bug and would projectile vomit all over them. Plastering on a phony smile, I wound my way around tables and waiters and arrived, feeling like an invasion force. Blondie stared up at us like we were selling Avon.

Bob looked like a fox caught in the henhouse, but he said, "Hi. Why don't you join us? This is Jennifer, Dr. Jennifer Jonas, another ER junkie. Jen, meet my neighbors, Maureen and Susan."

We said hello while I thought, *Just a neighbor, of course, what else, stupid?*

Then Susan jumped in with, "Should I call you Dr. Jonas, in case we meet next time with me on a gurney?"

She assured us *Jen* would be fine.

"So, Jen. Are you married?" Susan's favorite first question lately. I sunk into my seat and busied myself flagging down a waiter while giving Susan a warning kick.

"No. Medical school, interning, and the ER didn't leave much time for men and, truthfully, what's the point of marriage unless you want kids?"

That was TMI. Was she trying to let Bob know she wasn't the marrying kind? Or the childbearing kind? Susan was ready to enjoy herself, though. "So, you traded having children for a career?" she asked, a gleam in her eyes.

Bob interrupted the sudden female sharing by jumping up and saying, "Let's hit the buffet, ladies, before they're out of shrimp!" I stayed behind to order drinks for me and Susan; she loved the food-gathering challenge and I needed alcohol. I slugged down a frozen margarita so fast I had a bout of acute brain freeze. I was still grimacing with pain when Susan and Bob returned, enough food on his plate to feed a family. Dr. Jen carried a plate with three tiny shrimp and a taste of salad—happy hour buffet was wasted on her. We all tucked into our food—well, all except Jen, who nibbled daintily. I thought Bob was keeping his mouth full to avoid conversation.

A full mouth never slowed down Susan. "Jen, you on one of those new diets? I'm thinking of the stomach-stapling deal, but life would be so sad without buffets."

She answered in a monotone without making eye contact. "Not my specialty, stomach stapling."

Conversation, thankfully, ceased. Bob, who had polished off his food fast enough to choke a pig, said, "I've gotta run. Doing an extra shift tonight." The good doctor sprang up too. "Bye, ladies. Enjoy. Work calls me too." She had an amazing ability to speak at us without seeing us, rather like John's oncology surgeon.

After they left I ordered a rare second margarita. "So much for my cougar days. He acted like he couldn't wait to escape. And Dr. Jen was constantly touching him."

Susan shrugged. "Could have just been an awkward situation for him. Time will tell."

***

Wednesday morning, while I was forcing down my medicinal oatmeal, Alyssa emerged from her room ghostly pale and shaking badly. Her eyes were sunken with dark circles around them. "Mom, I've gotta get to my doctor today!" She grimaced, in obvious pain.

"If it's an emergency, I'll call my doctor. Is it the stomach flu?"

"Flu's over. But all the barfing and diarrhea threw off my meds completely...and I'm out of...of one of them."

"I'm sure my doctor can prescribe a few pills to get you through to Friday—that's when you have a plane ticket, right?"

"Trust me. I've gotta go now. I changed my reservation. Can you drive me to the airport in an hour?"

"First I'd like to know why my doctor couldn't help you?" I was both angry and terrified. Was she going to a doctor or a dealer?

"One of my meds, I told you, it's kinda experimental. Your doc won't be able to prescribe it...it requires a special license."

"I'd like to come with you to this doctor."

She let out an anguished moan. "Not this time. Maybe later." She doubled over a chair, sweat pouring off her.

"Alyssa. I'm taking you to the ER right this minute."

"No! This is just 'cause I'm out of meds—I've got half a pill left to take before the flight so I won't be sick then. If you won't take me, I'll call a car service."

She went to her room and I followed. She got out her laptop and started Googling car services—she'd never get one in an hour.

"Alyssa, will the pill you have left be enough to get you through to your doctor and a pharmacy? The airline won't let you on board in your condition."

"I'll take it now. The flight's in two hours. We should go soon—please. Trust me."

If she said "trust me" one more time, I'd explode. She stayed in the bathroom for fifteen minutes while I paced. Once she emerged, the pill had already worked wonders. I drove to the airport with Alyssa in the back seat, still wriggling a bit in pain but no longer emitting guttural groans. I tried hard to concentrate on the traffic so we wouldn't both have to be pried out of my Prius. At Jet Blue departures, Alyssa got out with her backpacked computer, looked in my window and said, "Thanks for trusting me," then pulled herself up and walked like an old woman toward the automatic doors. I wanted to jump out and help her, but I knew I couldn't, so I sat there and cried, with runny nose and eyes, until a security guy came over, tapped on my window, and told me to move on.

Chapter 8

It took me over two hours to drive home from the airport—not only heavy traffic, but I had to stop and blow my nose and wipe my eyes twice. Bright sun plus dark sunglasses plus tears equals driving blind. At home, when I stepped out of the elevator, I looked down the open corridor toward my end unit and saw a very tall man with a huge barrel chest in front of my porch door. He had a long black ponytail and he was trying to jimmy my lock with a card. He turned and looked toward me. A loud yelp escaped from my mouth and I jumped back into the elevator, banging on the "door close" button, scrabbling around until I got 911 on my cell. I was giving my name and address to the 911 operator, in a panic-stricken voice, when the elevator door opened at the bottom. Bob was standing there—what a reassuring sight! I grabbed his arm and pulled him into our clubhouse.

"My God, Maureen, what's wrong?"

Thankfully, the clubhouse was empty. I was shaking, and blurted out in machine-gun mode, "A huge guy, ugly—he was breaking into my porch door. Police are on the way." I was breathing like a marathoner on her last lap. "And Alyssa, she's in New York—I think she's an addict!" I reached high C with the last word. Bob opened his arms and I fell into them, shaking, but fear kept more tears away.

"Let's wait in the parking entrance so we can see the police coming. We can watch the elevator door from a distance." He put his arm around my waist and propelled me forward. We walked this way past the pool and I saw Leo, hands on hips, staring at us as we moved quickly on. It took ten minutes for the police to arrive, and my fear escalated each minute we stood out there at the entrance—glad I wasn't under attack. After retelling my story to the cops, one of them took the emergency stairs and the other went up "old creaky." They were back in a few minutes.

The tall Hispanic officer said they saw no one and my door was still locked. "But there were some new scratches in the paint around you door lock, so someone was there," he stated. They rang the doorbells of the three nearest neighbors; no one answered and all the doors were locked. Whoever it was must have slipped down the fire stairs and out the back on foot. They'd look around.

Bob said, "I'll come to your apartment with you and stay for a while, unless you want to stay at my place till you feel better."

"Please come to my place. I need some company right now." I was still shaking, adrenaline flooding my brain. My too-quiet life— how could it have reversed in just one week? Boredom beckoned like nirvana. When we unlocked my porch and then my main door, I made sure I relocked both behind me. I rarely locked my porch when I was home, but "new rule," as Bill Maher would say.

We sat side by side on my white leather sofa. Bob took my hand—in a supportive way. "You look like you haven't slept; your eyes are red and, I'll bet you don't know it, but your shirt's on inside-out."

I looked down at my seams showing, the pocket flipped out, and had to laugh—then started half-laughing, half-crying, also known as hysteria. Bob went into the kitchen and brought out a tall glass of water. I thought he was going to pour it on me.

"Drink!" he commanded. "I think you're dehydrated."

I drank and calmed down.

"What happened with Alyssa—did she tell you about her addiction?"

I told him everything that had happened over the past week, culminating in Alyssa's total breakdown that morning.

"Well, it could be withdrawal from a legal medication. If her shrink had her on any of the benzodiazepines and she lost all her fluids and ran out, that could give her those symptoms, but a drug that needs a special license—the only one I can think of is Suboxone and it is *only* used to treat recovering opiate addicts." He leaned over and patted my shoulder. "It's hard to find a new doctor who will prescribe Suboxone. Not just the license business. Ah, it's complicated."

I felt a chill run through my body. "An opiate addict. You do mean a pill addiction, like Oxycontin not, God forbid, heroin?"

"Afraid there's not much difference, except with pills you don't risk dirty needles or having poisons mixed in."

"What should I do? What *can* I do?"

"I'd advise an intervention. I've been part of a few."

"A what?"

"When she comes back, have a group of close friends, relatives, and maybe a shrink come over, and ask her to explain what's going on. Then, if you can afford it, maybe you can convince her to go into rehab—unless you want to be her rehab facility."

"I can't absorb all this. I need to know more. And I need sleep, but I'm spooked—that strange man at my door."

"Listen. I'll be at work for the next eight hours. You can sleep in my guest room. I have an alarm system—my mother used to regularly set it off by mistake. Get whatever you need to bring over."

"Thanks. Let me grab my iPhone, just in case, and my purse."

I felt like an invalid. Bob held my arm as I locked up my apartment and we walked next door.

First he showed me how to set his alarm system, then led me to his guest room. "You'll be fine after a nap. And make sure you eat something. See you when I get back from work." He patted my back as I sat down with a sigh.

***

I slept at Bob's for most of the afternoon and evening, after leaving voice and email messages with Susan and Alyssa to call my cell if they needed me. When I woke, I found a note from Bob on the fridge telling me to stay until he got home and insisting I eat his leftover stir-fry. I was ravenous by then and polished off his garlic chicken—so spicy my lips were burning—followed by a huge dish of Ben & Jerry's Cherry Garcia to cool my mouth. I watched some ghastly police dramas on his mammoth wide-screen TV, once I figured out how to turn it on. I was certain the TV was not his mother's.

A little after midnight the sound of Bob's door opening woke me up from my sofa-nap and I screamed—I couldn't figure out where I was for a few seconds—then laughed, then started to cry again. Another bout of hysteria. Maybe *I* needed rehab.

"Maureen. Sorry I frightened you. How can I help?"

"It's just so awkward…this whole mess…and involving you. I'm sorry."

He sat next to me and took my hand. "If you're not too sleepy, I want to tell you my sad story. I've shared this with very few people. Do you feel up to listening to *my* mess?"

I nodded a yes. He continued to hold my hand and told me about his high life in New York City—he was one of those rich traders, a Master of the Universe: big house in Darien, a pied-à-terre in the city, making obscene amounts of money, drinking too much, partying with cocaine always available in the bathrooms.

"My ex-wife is from a poor family and she went crazy with all the money—worse than me. But we both loved Suzanne, our daughter, and we kept her life pure and perfect. When Suzanne was fifteen— what a beauty she was—I picked her up from her friend's house about eleven one night. I'd been at a party, had a few drinks, a few hits. It was winter and the roads were icy."

His voice was cracking, his two hands now held my one, and he was trembling. "I was probably going too fast—I don't even remember. The car went off the road, hit a pole, rolled down an embankment. The ambulance...the ER...I watched them take Suzanne in for surgery, doctors and nurses and tubes surrounding her gurney. They stopped me at a door, had to have a guard hold me back. She never regained consciousness. My wife never spoke to me again."

He had started to cry, that stifled male version. This time I opened *my* arms. I did not know what to say; I patted his back, uttered some platitudes. I was holding him in a tight embrace, rocking him like a hurt child, when we tumbled over on the sofa. Bob landed on top of me. He began gently whispering in my ear, "Thank you, Maureen. You're a good listener—I trust you." My ear was on fire. I could feel his chest convulsing on top of mine as he tried to pull himself together. Then he began to kiss that hot ear.

Within seconds, I felt his pelvis moving against mine and mine automatically responding; his mouth moved on, busy kissing my lips, my throat. His deep baritone voice moaned, "Maureen, oh, Maureen."

All the emotions of the last week, the last twenty-four hours, welled up inside me and a dam burst. Now that old signal was a five-alarm fire, and I suddenly wanted body-slamming, wild sex. Somehow we both knew it—without any words—and started tearing clothes off each other. His mouth sucked and probed every part of me, not slowly, but with sirens full blast. I had a nagging worry my vagina would be too dry from lack of use, but his tongue eliminated that fear. I heard myself scream words I had not used in many years.

We lay spent and stunned on his mother's chintz sofa, a stupid Aflac duck commercial quacking on TV, the smell of sex a fog around us. "You okay, Maureen? I hope I didn't hurt you or, I don't know, take advantage of you. Believe it or not, I've been celibate since I—"

"It's been four or five years for me, and…maybe I took advantage of you!"

We both laughed. "I'll get you a robe. And how about a brandy?" He was standing right over me; his body was sturdy and muscular, a bit bowlegged; his genitals hovered five inches above my face—I couldn't stop myself from looking. I felt warm and moist and sexy and thirsty and my skin was prickly all over. On top of that, I had the unbelievable urge to clamp my mouth around his damp penis—the first circumcised one I'd seen. *Oh my God, how have I gone from avoiding men and sex to fucking?* I pulled his mother's afghan over most of my nakedness, especially my soft belly and naked pudenda.

"Yes. A brandy. And lots of cold water. Please." I watched him walk into his bedroom—no old, sagging butt there. He tossed me a white terry robe and I quick-stepped to the bathroom to pee. I prayed I wasn't damaged.

In his mother's pretty pink bathroom, I stared at the sexy, still-panting stranger in the mirror. My face had a rosy glow; my lips were swollen and my eyes puffy. I cleaned my body of his fluids, suddenly realizing I'd never even thought about a condom. And he was the goddamn nurse. Why didn't he...?

I guess I'd been fooling myself for years; my body had far different ideas about sex than my mind. I was feeling a combination of lethal embarrassment and total awe. I was still a functioning sexual being but didn't want to be. It still felt like adultery to me. *Get your head together and live in the moment, for heaven's sake.*

When I got back, he had brandy, water, and brownies on the coffee table. The TV was turned off, and Peggy Lee singing "Fever" filled the room—too appropriate a song.

"Bob, this song, I—"

"Sorry." He actually blushed. "I forgot—first one on this playlist." We sipped and listened.

There was no way I could chew and swallow a brownie. My brain was in chaos as thoughts flung themselves around. When an instrumental piece started, I told Bob, "I'm not ready to talk about what just happened and I'm still afraid to go home, so...can I sleep in your guest room tonight? Alone, of course."

He moved closer—he'd put on silk boxer shorts and a T-shirt. I almost woofed! His muscles bulged and he had a perfect six-pack. After watching old men at the pool, watching Bob enthralled me. Kissing the top of my head, he agreed we'd both better get some sleep and promised to wake me for breakfast. "You're an amazing woman, Maureen. Tonight was a surprise for both of us, I think. I just hope it was as good for you as it was for me!"

That sounded like a line from a sixties movie, but I answered, "It was. Good night."

I lay there in Bob's guest bed, my mind and body struggling to catch up with each other. The last time I'd had that kind of sex was about ten years ago when John and I went on a vacation to St. Croix. We'd always joked about having "hotel sex." I would never have had premeditated sex with Bob, but it had been so unexpected—and cathartic, perhaps. Afterwards, the logical me was ready to beat up the emotional me, but sleep—a swirling, roiling sleep—shut down my internal debate.

***

I woke to the smell of bacon—is there anyone who doesn't salivate from that aroma? I slipped into the guest bathroom and did my best to repair my face and hair. My purse always contained a few basic fixes. When I emerged wearing my wrinkled clothes from the day before, right-side out at least, Bob had coffee, eggs, and bacon ready at the kitchen counter. He was dressed in shorts and a form-fitting tee, so I could watch his muscles ripple as he moved about the kitchen—I was not sure my old heart, to say nothing of the rest of me, would hold out.

He greeted me with a hearty, "Good morning, Maureen. Hope you like a big breakfast."

I smiled and nodded. "I force-feed myself oatmeal most mornings, which I truly hate, so this is a treat."

As usual, he had a jazz group playing softly in the background. He poured coffee and he had real cream, something I loved but rarely allowed in my house. Bob said he was meeting friends to go kayaking and would be gone all morning. "Do you want to stay here?"

I told him I wanted to go home and I would find a company to come and put in an alarm system, hopefully later that day. As we ate, we were rather shy with each other. I kept my eyes on my eggs and my comments on the food. He kept up a dance: moving plates, then pots, salt and pepper, cream and sugar. Neither of us brought up last night's hot sex. It felt like a dream—except I woke to an unusual soreness in my crotch and was amazed to find two hickeys on my neck.

As he was cleaning up—he wouldn't let me help—he surprised me with, "I'm selling this condo. Just put in on the market."

"Well, you're way too young for the crowd here. Even I'm a bit on the young side for the Gardens."

Bob sat back down after refilling his cup, then asked, "How old are you, if you don't mind my asking?"

I did mind, but I wasn't one of those women who tried to keep her age a secret. "I'm sixty-nine. Next one's a milestone—ugh!"

Bob choked on his coffee, spitting some back into his cup. "No!" He looked shocked—did he suddenly realize he'd *shtupped* grandma? "I...I figured you were about fifty-eight, sixty tops. You don't look your age and your daughter's so young."

"Yeah. I was one of the older mommies at 'Mommy and Me' classes."

Watching Bob's face try to deal with my ancientness was almost funny. He'd try to smile, then chuckle a little, then look away and take another sip of coffee. "You are okay, right?" he said, in a new, nervous voice.

I wanted to add to his shock by telling him I had herpes, but instead responded with, "Of course. I'm not out to pasture yet."

Bob looked pale and awed as he walked me into my apartment. He gave me a chaste hug goodbye. "Call me on my cell if you need anything at all, anytime. I have it on vibrate when I'm at work. I'll be back by 1:00 today."

Chapter 9

After Bob left, I closed and locked my hurricane shutters—no one could break through those. With my apartment barricaded, I felt safe enough to get naked and take a fast shower. When I checked my calendar afterwards, I ratcheted up my curse-meter. I had forgotten that at least six women were due at my apartment at two o'clock.

My monthly UU spirituality group (we called it BYOT, or Build Your Own Theology) was very important to me, and it was too late to cancel, so I quickly cleaned up the apartment, dug out some snacks, and chilled some Pinot Grigio. The topic for the meeting was Sylvia Boorstein's book, *Pay Attention, For Goodness' Sake*, with easy-to-follow meditations. Given the past week, I had not read one word, but certainly could use some meditation instead of medication. Our discussions usually ended with wine and cheese—were wine and meditation at odds?

A phone call to our maintenance man, Julio, got quick results. His cousin would install an alarm system that afternoon—Julio had heard about the police visit yesterday. The installation, he assured me, would be quick and easy, since only two of my windows faced the porch; the rest were unreachable by would-be assaulters.

I checked my email and Alyssa had responded, saying she was going to stay with a friend for a couple of days and, not to worry, she was fine. *Yeah, don't worry, like don't breathe.* Finally, I called Susan. "Girlfriend, I am almost ready to be committed. Can you come over for Chinese takeout tonight?"

"You betcha! Got your message about not being at home yesterday but, ahem, your car was still here! Good old Leo asked me about you every time I ran into him. And the place's buzzin' about you and the police. I'm feelin' very left out!" She sounded angry with me. Or maybe just suspicious.

***

By 2:15 my six "spiritual" buddies were sitting around my dining area table. I lit our candle and Millie read some words for centering: "We come together to gain strength from each other, to use that strength to help others, to strengthen our connections with the cosmos. Blessed be."

We then did our usual check-in and each of us shared a recent happy or sad event in our lives. As the hostess, I would go last, and I listened as everyone shared happy events, ending with Millie, whose forty-year-old daughter was pregnant—she'd about given up on either of her two kids ever reproducing. She beamed with joy.

Janice chimed, "Your turn, Maureen." I had just put a pitcher of water and glasses on the table.

"I…I've had a very difficult week…it was so bad I don't want to ruin our meditation talk, 'cause I'm gonna need meditation or I'll OD on Valium soon."

Millie, our de facto leader, said, "Let's do a shorter version of our discussion, practice a meditation, and then we'll listen to Maureen over wine."

All agreed. I barely listened to the discussion, my mind and heart elsewhere, worry trumping all. We practiced a lovely and easy meditation and I did feel more relaxed and more connected to the group—I felt safe with them around me. Just after the meditation, Julio's cousin arrived to start installing the alarm system. He had to ask me a few questions. That got everyone's attention.

"Well, Maureen. Out with it!" said Millie. She had a commanding voice, which she used when she occasionally filled in for our minister and delivered her own sermons. I think Millie was at least seventy-five, but she had the energy and zest for life of a forty-year-old.

I gave them a rundown of my week, leaving out, of course, doing the deed with Bob. I did weave in my cougar date with the trauma— guess I was showing off that I'd been asked out. By the time I told them about my ride to the airport with Alyssa, I was trying hard not to weep again—enough was enough of the damn waterworks. I finished off describing the attempted break-in. Every woman around my table looked shocked and saddened and frightened.

The shyest member of our group, Sylvia, a pretty fifty-something lady from Long Island, grabbed my hand, and Millie put her arm around me. Sylvia said in a whispery voice, "You and I should meet soon, if...if you want to. I went through something like this with my youngest son." She started to cry and finally got out, "He's dead, died of an overdose—but maybe I can help you."

Everyone looked weepy as they hugged and comforted Sylvia. She had never shared that before. Then Millie said, "Let's all hold hands around the table. Maureen, I know I speak for all of us: we'll help in any way we can. And, remember, everything said in this group, we know, stays in the group."

Hands squeezed, tears dried, the rest of our conversation was subdued. Soon Julio's cousin needed my attention, so everyone said quick goodbyes except Sylvia. She and I made a date to have lunch the next day. Later I got instructions on how to use my new alarm system, which seemed quite simple, as long as I remembered to quickly punch in my code when I came in each time.

I flopped down on top of my bed for a short nap, feeling secure with my new alarm set and warmed by thinking about all the kind and helpful words from my group. As much as I appreciated my church group, Susan was still the best thing in my life. I believed she had moved to Florida to save me from self-inflicted isolation after John's death. I would be forever grateful that she decided to stay and sell her apartment in New York.

I woke to my doorbell bonging away, shuffled to the door, and peered out, afraid I'd see Mr. Ponytail, but it was Susan standing with one hand on her hip and one poking the bell. I could not stop myself from thinking of the nursery song "I'm a Little Teapot." How long had she been hitting the doorbell? I was still groggy—afternoon wine-nap—and rushed to the porch to let her in. As I opened the main door, death-to-eardrum sounds filled the apartment and I ran back to the box and punched in my code. When I finally got Susan to come in, the phone rang, and it was the alarm company. I told the guy on the phone that I thought I could open the door from the inside without setting off the alarm. The company rep laughed and said I always needed to enter the code to open the door when the alarm was set. Oops.

"Damn, Maureen. What the hell is happening here?"

I filled her in on Alyssa's emergency trip, telling her how I was quite sure my daughter was addicted to Oxycontin or Vicodin.

"Oy, I always thought she was smarter than that. Taking something so dangerous, just to get high; it's so stupid, and..." For the first time ever, Susan was out of words, and she hugged me—she was not a hugger either, so I felt how much she cared.

"And that's not all!" I was getting shrieky again. *Cool it.* "I saw a really big and scary-ugly man trying to break into my apartment yesterday, when I got back from the airport. I called the police; they found nothing, just a scratched lock. But Bob saw how terrified I was and—"

"Eh! Now that's *mushugana*. Isn't it possible this Mr. Ugly had the wrong apartment?"

"Then why did he disappear—without a trace? Bob and I were out front waiting for the cops—he didn't go by." I was getting angry. "And I know what I saw!"

"Okay, okay. I'm just thinkin'. It doesn't make sense. Tell me what he looked like?"

I described him and how Bob rescued me and put me up for the night, leaving out the *shtupping* part, but she eyed me shrewdly and a little grin replaced her severe look.

"Well, Reenie, I'll make sure the Board circulates his description and have residents call me if they see him, or maybe someone knows him. And you now have a nice, safe—and very loud—alarm system. So let's order before I faint from hunger."

We ordered our usual from Wok It Out, and their delivery came so fast, I had to think they were mind readers and were waiting outside. Susan set the table and sipped wine while I arranged those wonderful little white boxes with the metal handles, then we dug in. To lighten the moment, Susan told me one of her horde of Jewish-Chinese food jokes. "So, do ya know why Jewish women love Chinese food? Cause *won ton* spelled backward is 'not now.'"

I chuckled, but soon returned to my misery-mood.

"Guess it's not a joking time, but ya gotta keep up your spirits. Do what you can for Alyssa, but take care of yourself too."

"Susan, honestly, I've been obsessing lately and don't know if I ever really wanted to have children—and yesterday, Alyssa said she thought I never wanted her. I feel like a shitty failure of a mother."

Sue looked me straight in the eyes. "Stop that right now! I've known you for forever and you were, well, a little shell-shocked when you found yourself knocked up, but you were great with Alyssa—all those long vacations at Long Beach Island, skiing together—you did it all, sweetie."

"But if my heart wasn't a hundred percent there, would she have felt that?"

"Look. It was probably the last eight years that separated you two emotionally. After all, she lost her dad and you lost your husband, and from a long, ghastly illness..."

"Thank you, Sue. I don't know what I'd do without you."

"You'd probably be hanging out with Bob or Leo—that's what I'm thinkin'—and I'm maybe a little jealous sometimes. But I don't know what I'd do without you either." She had the start of a tear in one eye—Susan did not cry. She was a rock.

After a pause she sat up straighter and said, "I have a big secret too. I've been on a big and beautiful web dating service and my first date in the modern era—for coffee—is tomorrow. We've been emailing for a few weeks. He's short, round, bald, and a Jew from New York and he's seen my unretouched photos. I'm not even nervous." She tittered. Nervously, I thought.

"That's great. I assume he's retired. What did he do before Florida?"

"My mother will be cheering from her grave—he ran a successful hedge fund. Sounds like he's rolling in dough—not that I give a hoot about his money."

We chatted about Susan's fund-man. She and Michael had been burning up cyberspace, sharing about five emails a day. Wonderful news, so why was I suddenly feeling dread? Was it fear of no longer being Susan's *numero uno*—had I become that selfish? Or had I become that dependent?

Chapter 10

Early Friday morning I dragged myself to Anika's yoga studio. It was her calming, restorative yoga class where we draped or curled our bodies over large bolsters and used blocks to hold up our inverted postures. Anika bowed to me, hands at heart center. "Maureen. I rarely see you at this class. Are you injured?"

"No. But I've been under a lot of stress recently and I remembered how comforting this class can be."

Later, lying twisted over a bolster, I opened my eyes to see Leo staring at me. His head should have been twisted the other way— didn't he know left from right? I immediately closed my eyes and ignored him for the rest of class. Having him right next to me made me self-conscious in my body-hugging yoga togs—and my new top revealed "headlights."

As we rolled up our mats he asked, "How are you? I've been worried about you and your daughter. Let's have breakfast—my treat. Please?"

His eyes showed concern and I agreed to meet him at the Blue Goddess, then worried Susan's date might be there that morning, but the terrace was empty when I arrived. Leo was waiting at the counter where we ordered lattés and scones and gorgeous fresh strawberries. We sat outside at my favorite table, just enough sun hitting it to be comfortable. We both sipped, buttered, commented on the weather and the yoga class. I studied him as he ate. His face reminded me of statues I'd seen in Italy—a strong profile, a very Roman nose, an attractive visage. His curly silver hair framed his face.

I heard Leo rumble, clearing his throat in that overture some men use before getting serious. "I haven't seen your daughter in a few days, and I was upset when I heard about your intruder. Ah, how can I help?"

Where to start? I gave Leo the abbreviated—that is, sexless—version of recent events.

"What have you heard from Alyssa?"

"She said she's staying with friends for a few days, but she doesn't answer my emails and her cell goes to voice mail saying, 'Mailbox full.'" I sighed. "I'm terrified, but what can I do?" The effects of yoga were still shielding me from severe agita. "I'm meeting a friend today whose son had a drug problem. Not sure if this visit won't notch up my stress—her son ODed, died!"

Leo frowned, his gray and white eyebrows almost joining over his nose, his face affected by our mutual pain. "Honestly, Maureen, when my son was addicted and went through rehab—twice—I needed to talk to a psychologist for a while. I couldn't communicate with my son and I was worried and angry and frustrated. My shrink helped a lot."

"How's your son doing now?"

"He was lucky. Got it all back together, although an addict is never cured." Leo looked at the palm trees and his eyes dampened. "Our relationship is tenuous. We *talk* on eggshells. In the past, we both said things that left suppurating wounds." Leo stared into his coffee. His anguish was radiating out in waves.

A long minute later, he cleared his throat again. I was getting used to his style. "Changing the subject. My grandson's bar mitzvah is next Saturday and I would really like you to come with me. I can promise too much food and many laughs, and laughter is medicine we both need."

"I'd be terrible company. Who knows what could happen in a week. If my last week is any indicator, I expect a tsunami, at least."

"If we get a tsunami, then you're off the hook. But it will be a beautiful party and the ceremony is quite moving."

I paused. A happy, celebratory party might be a good prescription. "Okay. It sounds wonderful and I've attended some amazing bar mitzvahs in New Jersey—I love the way the whole family is included on the *bimah*." His eyebrows went up when I said *bimah*. "Remember, Susan has been my best friend for over fifty years—that makes me part Jewish!"

Leo put his hand over mine on the table—this time I did not yank it away. "Thank you, Maureen."

***

When I got home, I barely had time to shower and check email (none from Alyssa even though my last email was marked "High Priority"). *Shit!* I knew she checked her email constantly. I needed to learn to text. I was still a bit smartphone-challenged. I touched the envelope icon on my phone, touched the "new message" symbol, and typed, *Hi. Please get in touch. I'm having anxiety attacks. Love, MOM.* I knew texting was her generation's main communication method.

At one o'clock I arrived at Sylvia's apartment, which was on the twelfth floor of a grand new high rise overlooking the ocean. Wow. It shouted "top one percent." The doorman located my name, called ahead, then led me to the elevator. It did not clunk! And it opened right into her apartment. Not apartment, but a one-floor palace. I never knew shy Sylvia had megabucks. She dressed in a quiet, conservative fashion—no designer clothes, none of the Lauderdale-sized jewelry that weighed down many local dowagers.

Sylvia gave me a quick hug and led me to her terrace overlooking the Atlantic. Lunch was set on a glass table topped with pots of red cyclamen. "Is outside okay? It's a little breezy but warm, I think."

"It's perfect. And breathtaking!"

Sylvia smiled, then gave a timid laugh. "I married well, Maureen, or else I'd be living on a teacher's pension." She looked stricken, like she just realized I might be living on my teacher's pension.

I smiled. "I live well on my teacher's pension, plus monies from properties my husband and I sold—before the economy tanked, luckily."

We helped ourselves to Waldorf chicken salad and warm sourdough rolls, and jabbered about the inconsequential moments of life. Everyone starts with chitchat as warm-up before heading into emotional minefields. Eventually Sylvia said, "I know what you're going through with your daughter. Ten years ago, when I learned about my son's addictions, he'd already moved to injecting heroin—heroin is cheaper than pills. And easier to get. I offered to send him to the best rehab facility in the U.S., and he agreed to go. Everything was set up; the van would pick him up in Brooklyn the next Monday morning. But he wanted one last high—his friend told me this. He ODed that night." Sylvia sipped her tea then blew her nose into a lace-edged hankie. "My husband had a fatal heart attack the next week. I ended up in a facility with an emotional breakdown."

I was speechless. Frozen. I had to sip my tea to get moisture into my mouth—my tongue had stuck to my teeth. I finally answered, "I don't know what to say. You must have gone through such hell. I—"

"I'm okay now. It took a lot of therapy. I started a non-profit five years ago to help educate parents of junior and senior high kids. Vulnerable kids start taking drugs early. Also, we go into colleges with drama therapy—role-playing scenarios. Drama has an emotional impact on students."

"It sounds like you've channeled your grief in a positive way. You're amazing."

"And I know a group you should join. It's called Families Anonymous, or FA."

"Ugh. It sounds like AA or NA."

"It follows a similar format, but everyone in FA has a loved one who is an addict. They will tell you over and over in many ways that it's not your fault and there is very little you can do. One of their quotes is 'release with love.' I'll go with you if you want to try it out."

FA sounded painful and emotionally draining, but Sylvia sounded so sincere and so knowledgeable. *WTF, as my daughter often emails.* "Thanks. I'll go. And maybe I can help with your non-profit— just not yet."

"Well, like all non-profits, we're always fundraising. And you'd be good at that."

We hugged good-bye, holding tightly for an extra minute. We were both fighting tears but it was obvious Sylvia wanted to help to me. And maybe Leo would want to help her non-profit.

***

Back in my tiny-by-Sylvia-standards apartment, I paced up and down the living room—I could not sit, did not want Valium—pace, pace, pace, flip-flops flapping. Finally, I called Susan but had to leave a message. I wanted to hear about her first date (I could not remember Susan going on a date in decades) but also wanted a distraction from my brain spasms. I spent the rest of the day reading the book on meditation and practicing relaxing breathing methods. It would probably take years to get that breathing and mind-emptying stuff to work for me, but it was worth a try. There sure was a lot of shit I wanted to empty out of my brain-closets. Some people, especially men, seemed to be able to shut those closets and move on with the pleasures in life, appearing unaffected by the screaming behind those closed doors.

I decided to email Alyssa again.

To: Alyssa Manning

Subject: DEFCON 5

Al—Just hit Reply and let me know you're okay. Better yet, call me. Better yet, come back to Florida, please. Love, MOM

On Sunday there was still no reply from Alyssa, but Susan had emailed and asked to meet me at the pool after lunch. I made the mistake of looking into Alyssa's room again and the mess told me she must have been planning to come right back. I started to bite my nails—for the first time in sixty years. Buying a pack of cigarettes began to appeal to the un-meditative me. Damn. Even my UU service that morning with my favorite minister had not calmed me down. The subject line of DEFCON in my email to Alyssa had always been our code for "Mom needs to hear from you now."

When I got to the pool, Susan was in the water. *Huh?* Hanging on to the side, doing kicks—exercise! She got out, dried off, and sat next to me, in a regular chair, not her usual reclining one—and she was wearing a new bathing suit that made her look slimmer.

"You look terrific, Sue."

She smiled, really a Mona Lisa grin. "You haven't been too observant lately—I've lost twenty pounds in the last two months. Only need to lose about fifty more! But I'm feeling better already."

Did this correspond to the beginning of her email relationship with Mr. Hedge-fund? (What was his name?) Maybe the diet and the dating website came from a new determination to improve her health. I hoped so. "So how was your coffee date with the rich guy?"

"Well...well, we talked for over two hours. Then it was time for lunch. So we ordered food. Then we both went home—to our own homes—to rest and then meet for dinner. You know the place we both love right on the ocean? He's got pull! We had the best table! And, well, we have everything in common. We were both New York lifers who decided weather trumps Manhattan now. And his younger brother has an accounting firm and another brother is with J.P. Morgan and—oh my God, I can't shut up. I'm seeing him again tonight. Is that rushing things too much?"

"At our age, there is no rushing it."

"And we're both on diets. And we're gonna walk together every morning on the boardwalk and..."

My distress at this last statement must have shown on my face. I had not said a word.

"Maureen. Not really every day. You and me, we'll still meet at the Goddess twice a week."

"Hey. Don't worry about me." Thinking, I know I'm too selfish, but please do worry about me. Susan had spoiled me my whole adult life by always being available—never married, no children, rarely dated. My family had become her family, her preferred holiday destination. Sometimes John was a bit jealous of Sue and sometimes, I think, she was jealous of his hold on me.

"Go for it. But save me at least one morning a week. And I want to meet him."

"Sure, sure. But not too soon. 'Here's my younger, slimmer, prettier friend.' Not yet. Enough! I sound like a teenager already."

I told her about Sylvia and not hearing from Alyssa. She patted my hand and then ran off to the hairdresser. She did seem like a teen in love. And I felt abandoned—how stupid. I hoped her Internet friend was not a schmuck. I'd personally castrate him if he hurt Susan.

Chapter 11

Sunday evening I was in the middle of stir-frying vegetables when my telephone rang, so I ignored the call until I heard, "Call from Bob Gold-man," emanating in my phone's voice. Damn, I suddenly remembered he had left a message asking me to go to a Cuban jazz club—eek—tonight. And I never answered him. And I did not want to talk to him. "Call from Bob Gold-man," repeated, then the voice mail kicked in. His deep, sexy voice filled the kitchen.

"Hi...Maureen? About the jazz group tonight, I'm sorry, but I have to call it off. Something's come up."

His voice sounded gruff, not his usual mellow tones. I'd seen him duck into the clubhouse twice to avoid running into me. *Good!* For the past few days, I'd been feeling twinges in my nether regions whenever I walked—they say a sexual dry spell of five years re-virginizes your body. Thankfully my smart female gynecologist had put me on an estrogen cream many years ago or my banging with Bob might have left me bowlegged. I had not run into him since our breakfast of champions on Thursday and dreaded finding myself alone with him in our old creaky elevator. And I would never forget the shocked look on his face when he found out I was sixty-nine. His mouth kept making those movements like he'd eaten something vile and had no way to spit it out. Wednesday's sex had felt like an out-of-body experience at the time, and still did! I had no one I felt comfortable discussing it with, and that kind of discomfort was usually a good sign you screwed up.

***

Monday I decided to shop for a new dress for the bar mitzvah, hoping it would clear my head from obsessing about Alyssa and Bob. I peeked into the corridor first to avoid running into Bob and made it down the elevator alone, then slunk over to my Prius carport parking spot. *Whew, made it—no Bob.* I knew he was avoiding me too. Twice I saw him turn abruptly back to his car so we would not have to share an elevator ride and I watched him head for the fire stairs a few times. Well, at least I knew I looked young for my age.

I was about to step into my car when I saw Mr. Ugly skulking not ten feet away, leaning on a post, all six-foot-something of him. *Holy shit!* He was ambushing me. My brain went totally blank and I couldn't move a muscle. I forced myself to turn and start to run back when he shouted, "Please! Wait! I just need to talk to you about Alyssa."

Oh my God! That stopped me in my tracks. I reversed again and he, thankfully, kept his distance. Maybe he knew where she was, or worse, maybe he'd kidnapped her, or—

He added, "It's okay. I'm a...a friend of your daughter's. Please, can you meet me at the Healthy Donut, around the corner? I'll wait outside."

He had the deepest voice I'd ever heard. Since he obviously knew Alyssa, I answered, "Okay. But I'm not driving you there!" but he'd already disappeared toward the street.

I jumped into my car, locked the doors, and headed out to meet him. Was I being foolish? My stomach thought so and was sending out acid signals so strong I munched three Tums in one block. When I pulled into the Donut's parking lot, I saw him at an outdoor table with one mug of coffee in his hand and another mug across from him.

When I arrived at the table, he said, "I got you one with cream—guessed you'd like cream like Alyssa does."

I stared, speechless. He was younger than I'd first thought, about thirty, and not ugly, just huge—a football linebacker with shoulders that did not need any pads, and he was missing a neck. Staring at his massiveness, I said, "So, you must lift weights?" Brilliant opening. I didn't even know his name.

"Yeah. I'm a personal trainer...and an artist." He scrutinized my face and I felt like an amoeba on a slide. "She looks like you...same eyes, same cheekbones. I see where she gets her beauty." He paused. "Sorry, I'm Quinton, Quinton Paynter. Didn't Alyssa mention me?'

"No. And why were you breaking into my porch? I should be dialing the police!"

"Whoa. When no one answered your doorbell, I figured I needed to get inside the porch to the main door and knock. I was totally exhausted that day—just drove seventeen straight hours. An old friend told me Alyssa came here to you." He put his head his hands and breathed in deeply a few times. "When the elevator opened and you screamed, I wasn't sure I was in the right place. And I stunk—all those hours in the car—"

"Stop! Damn. How do you know my daughter? Who the hell are you?" I must have shouted since two men at a nearby table turned to watch us.

"I'm your goddamn son-in-law!" He slumped, as much as six-foot-five and three hundred pounds can slump. His limp black ponytail accentuated his indoor-white skin. "She never told you? We were married nine months ago. When she started up again I gave her an ultimatum: 'Clean up or get out.' She cleaned up all right—cleaned out my savings account of eight grand and disappeared. That was four months ago. The couple of friends we have in common couldn't or wouldn't tell me where she went."

Now I slumped. "Quinton, you said 'started up again.' I'm in the dark here. You mean illegal drugs? She's an addict?"

Quinton spoke softly and looked as sad as I felt. He'd known and loved Alyssa since their senior year together at Pratt. He'd been horribly upset when she'd thrown him over for a con artist—a guy he knew was a dealer and a user. When the jerk dumped her about a year ago, she'd called Quinton. He said he never knew the extent of her addictions.

"I thought she was a recreational drug user, not that I approved of that. But she's been taking so much Vicodin since she got out of college, it's a miracle her liver hasn't been destroyed. I got her into an outpatient clinic in the city when she was in painful withdrawal and they put her on Suboxone, which works kinda like Methadone. She got her life back together, at least I thought so; she could work without missing due dates. We got married—probably not the best move on my part, but I thought I could help her and I still loved her. I still do."

Quinton got up suddenly and ran inside—I thought either to pee or have a private cry. Just when I thought my life couldn't get worse, up pops a surprise son-in-law. I was in shock. Alyssa had horrific problems. Obviously, she was also totally estranged from me. What daughter does not tell her mother she got married?

When Quinton sat back down, I said, "I think she's on Suboxone now, but she's never told me about any of this. Now she's disappeared. Not a good sign, right?"

"Well, when the clinic weaned her off Suboxone, she secretly started calling her dealers again. She augmented opiates with cocaine so she could work, flip-flopping between the two drugs, either doing life at warp-speed or drooling in front of the TV. When I found her practically bleeding to death from her nose, I gave her a few chances to get back to rehab but...shit, I had to throw her out. I know it sounds crazy, but I've been searching for her ever since."

I wanted to crawl into a hole and pretend the past few weeks had not happened. I wanted to make believe everything I just heard was a nightmare. Pinpricks of pain attacked every part of my body. How does horrible news cause such pain? My throat was so constricted I had to drink some coffee in order to speak. "Could she have spent all that money in just three or four months?"

"Yeah. Easy. She was up to fifteen or twenty pills a day plus the cocaine. Probably a hundred, two hundred a day, I'd guess."

I started weeping. My breath came in shorter and shorter gasps and my heart jumped around like a caged squirrel. Was I having a heart attack? I remembered Sylvia saying her husband died from a heart attack right after her son ODed.

"You okay?" my son-in-fucking-law asked. Why was I so angry with him? I wanted to pound on him, kick him, for what? For knowing so much about Alyssa?

Finally I asked, "How do I know you are who you say?"

He pulled out a paper and smoothed it on the table. "I brought this to show you. Just in case. Our marriage license. Just a City Hall ceremony."

It looked legitimate but anyone could create anything today. "Look, let's keep in touch, but I won't share anything about Alyssa, assuming I ever have anything to share, unless she agrees. Okay?"

We both made notes in our phones and shook hands when I got up. I left him looking like a forlorn giant at the little table. I continued on, unconsciously, to T.J. Maxx, my favorite discount store, but could not even think about a pretty dress or a party with my daughter MIA. And married! Without telling me. But maybe Quinton was the con artist and would ask me for money soon. I did not want to believe him.

Suddenly I had an overwhelming need to talk to John. He could always calm me down—he was my Valium. *But shouldn't I be an independent person by now?* I'd been a widow for over two years. Some of my friends acted like I was still stuck in my bereavement. I got teary when talking about John to a group at church last month and one woman actually told me, "It's time to turn off the waterworks, dear." That statement angered me so much the heat dried my tears right up. But it was true that my tear-duct mechanism had been in overdrive since John's death sentence eight years ago.

I returned home and spent the next day watching *Pride and Prejudice*, the good version with Colin Firth, followed by *Daniel Deronda* on Netflix. I was addicted to British period dramas. I didn't leave my apartment until Tuesday morning when I dragged my TV-drugged self to yoga to sweat out my demons. Exercise, my emotional balm. As I was leaving for yoga, Susan called. "Hey. Are we meetin' at the Goddess today? I got a lot to share."

***

Yoga, when it works, clears your brain. The struggle, the strength, and the endurance needed to move from one challenging position to another, to hold your quivering muscles in the pose, stops your monkey mind from dwelling on your problems. Well, that was the theory, but having a drug-addicted, secretly married daughter who was hiding out somewhere *killed* that theory right off. I could not keep my balance in any position. *Shit-shit-shit*, my mother's mantra, trumped *Om*.

When I walked into the garden at the Goddess, Susan jumped up and hugged me. "What's wrong, *bubala*? You look like *dreck*."

I told her about Mr. Ponytail, known as Quinton, and the extent of Alyssa's addiction problem, at least in the world-according-to-Quinton.

"Well, if this Quinton is on the up-and-up, it's worse than I imagined. What'll you do?"

"For starters, I think I'll go to an FA meeting with Sylvia. And maybe find a good talk therapist. Leo sort of suggested I do that."

"Then start right away. Don't wait to get professional help. We don't know *bupkis* about this addiction business."

I sat up straight and breathed deeply. I was always centered on my problems—probably ever since John's illness. How did anyone enjoy spending time with me? *Poor Susan, my cheerleader all these years.* I looked at her and asked, "How about you, Sue? Things are good with, ah, the fund guy?"

"Yeah. Actually great. We'll talk about Michael when you're feeling better."

We drank and ate in silence, each lost in thought, and hugged goodbye very early. I'd had more hugs from Susan the past week than in the past year.

Chapter 12

Tuesday night I ate my single-person dinner of scrambled eggs and wilted salad—Susan had cancelled out of our Happy Hour for the first time in ages. Still no sign of Alyssa. Her voice mail still said "mailbox full" and even my texts went unanswered. I'd never felt so bereft—a widow with a lost daughter and a best friend who was obviously embarking on an adventure without her. I did wish Sue well with her new romance...I did!

I needed to plan for my future. But right then I was so depressed that all I could think about was collecting pills and checking out before old age and senility overtook me. While watching my mother deteriorate at a nursing home, with Alzheimer's eating her brain, I'd vowed to not get warehoused for my final years.

The phone rang as I was cleaning up the dishes and I answered without screening—not like me at all. Bob's incredibly deep, resonating voice embraced me with "Hello there, Maureen."

I staggered. Why was he calling? He'd been avoiding me since our surprising sexual encounter on his sofa. "Oh! Hi, Bob."

"I wanted to ask how you're doing? With your daughter. I've been worried."

I blurted out, "Oh, well, it's terrible. I'm losing it." I told him the whole tale, including my misgivings about Quinton the bodybuilder. "What do you think about all this?"

"Damn. That's…well." There was a long silence. "I think I'd hire a detective. He could check out Quinton and also try to find Alyssa. I know a good guy in Brooklyn."

I took down the name and phone number of Bob's private eye. A new mommy-nightmare—spying on your adult child. Nasty stories from movie dramas washed over me—young women tortured by pimps, trapped by their addictions. Was investigating a good idea? Did I really want to know? Sylvia had already told me I couldn't help Alyssa—did I believe her? What would I do if the detective located Alyssa and she refused to speak to me? Could I legally kidnap her and spirit her off to a detox in the desert or rehab on a deserted island? I needed to learn more—lots more. I hated feeling so helpless.

Even in high school, Alyssa often managed to slip away from us. I remember sitting down with her during her junior year and listening to "Mom, just, y'know, back off."

"I can't—I'm your mother. I have to be sure you're safe."

"And you have to trust me. You can't follow me around every minute of every day. Jenny, y'know, she had sex in the janitor's closet at school—not with the janitor. Some girls I know smoke pot in the showers after gym. But, Mom, I'm not doing anything, just having fun."

I was never sure how much to limit her. John and I rarely argued, but we did have clashes how much freedom to grant Alyssa in high school. Maybe I should have hired a detective back then. But she was a straight-A student, on the tennis team, wrote for the school newspaper, and was voted president of the computer club. She couldn't have been taking drugs then, could she?

***

After a night of nightmares and night sweats, I staggered out of bed looking a lot like an addict myself: eyes bloodshot, hair standing up in clumps. At the click of nine, gripping my coffee, I called Sean O'Brien at the Brooklyn Apex Agency. At least I felt I was doing something other than constantly worrying, but it was still the most awkward phone call I'd ever placed. As I later emailed Sean all the information he'd asked for, including some pictures of Alyssa and a description of Quinton-the-huge, I became overwhelmed by misgivings.

I sat on my porch with my second cup of java lightened by lots of heavy cream I'd just splurged on—cream Quinton had known I craved. He'd noticed how much Alyssa and I look alike—something she hated to hear. Why do daughters usually cringe when told they look like or act like their mothers? I remembered hating to hear those comparisons to my own mother. I guess we spend so much energy separating from our moms that we don't want to risk reattachment. Or maybe we just don't want to picture ourselves getting old.

My cell rang and it was Sylvia insisting I go to an FA meeting with her that night. "Honestly, Maureen, it will help. I'll meet you in front of All Saints and we'll go up together." I reluctantly agreed.

***

From the moment we entered the church meeting room, I felt trapped. Pictures of old male ministers lined the wall of the overly warm room and at least ten people stared at me: the newbie. Most looked haggard or in pain—no smiles of welcome from this group.

As it was explained to me, each of us in the room had personal problems to examine. The evening's leader, Nancy, handed me a red book and we all took turns reading the Twelve Steps—very similar to what an addict would be reading at an AA or NA meeting. I resented the statement that *I* had to change. What did I have to do with Alyssa's problem? Moreover, I really was thrown by the stated need to believe in a *Power greater than ourselves*. The only step that made sense was the first: *We admitted we were powerless over drugs and other people's lives—that our lives had become unmanageable.*

Nancy announced, "The topic tonight is our need to be perfect and how this sometimes hurts those we love. Does anyone want to speak?"

We had already gone over the rules. You could only speak about your own experience and you must never give advice, interrupt, or make comments. One by one, most of the eleven people in the room spoke. Many had children with terrible problems: one dad had a kid in jail, another had a daughter going on trial. *Shit. Why did I come here?* I said nothing, just curled up into my chair.

The last person who spoke said, "My name is Harriet. My son James said he never wants to come home again, never, and I don't want him to come home again, ever. He told me my perfect life made his impossible to live. I'm an interior decorator, so I like beautiful things around me. James said I made him feel like a hopeless mess. One day he came home and stole all my jewelry, then threw dirt and dog poop all over my white living room. I felt raped. I had him arrested. Now I'm so depressed I want to burn my house down."

Harriet started to sob. One woman hugged her, another passed her the tissues, then everyone was silent for a few very painful minutes—no one raised their hands to speak after that.

Nancy motioned for us to stand up and asked us to hold hands and recite the *Serenity Prayer*. I could not wait to escape—holding hands with Mrs. Misery and Mr. Agony made my skin crawl, and the man next to me held my hand as though he was my personal savior, giving supportive squeezes throughout.

Sylvia had sensed my discomfort. When we were back in the parking lot she told me, "The meetings grow on you, really. And hearing it repeated, that you are helpless, helps."

"I get it, but I don't get what I'd get from continuing to go, that's all. Sorry. The talk about 'God as you experience him' doesn't work for me."

"I had trouble with that part too. Just trust me for a couple of sessions. Okay?"

Maybe I'd give it another try, only because Sylvia was such a believer in FA, but I would just listen. I had buried the discussion about being a perfectionist in a mind-closet. Both John and Alyssa had often told me I tried too hard to make everything in life perfect—that I would always feel disappointed by the people I loved.

Just before a dinner party when Alyssa was a toddler, I was in a frenzy trying to clean floors, cook, and make sure the powder room was free of potties. I'd been barking out orders to John like a drill sergeant all day.

Finally he hugged me close and said, "Maureen, no one will care if the house isn't perfect. That's not why they're coming over. Chill!" That did happen often—lace-curtain Irish neurosis—but it certainly didn't lead to Alyssa's problem. Did it?

***

By Thursday morning, I was ready for some transformative yoga, but the class was more challenging than usual. Anika tried to get us to balance with our knees on our forearms in crow pose and I fell forward onto my head. Leo was next to me and whispered, "I think you and I should pass on crow if we want to live." I had to laugh, which was a good release. We got a scolding look from Anika, who hated any commentary during her class.

While rolling up our mats, Leo suggested we meet again at the Goddess for coffee and goodies. I was starved, as I always was after yoga, since I had to do yoga on a totally empty stomach. A few weeks ago an early breakfast of oatmeal almost made a messy return during a long down-dog pose.

At the café, we ordered the same lattes and ginger scones from the same bored barista—I tried to pay but Leo beat me to it. Seated at the same cozy table, he asked how things were going. "Any tsunamis yet?"

"Well—the Maureen rollercoaster ride continues!" I told him, my ongoing grumbling painful to my own ears: the Quinton story, then about hiring my first detective, and my first FA meeting.

"Maureen. That's overwhelming! I'm sorry." He smiled and patted my shoulder. "Just remember—my son licked the problem." He took my hand. "What can I do to help?" He reminded me of Mr. Rogers on PBS—so sincere and direct. He was even wearing a little sweater. It was cool for early April and I wanted to borrow that sweater.

"I'm such a wreck. Do you really want me at your grandson's bar mitzvah?" I asked him, as I retrieved my hand.

"More than ever! My son, the one who had the drug problem, you'll meet him and see how things can change. And, well, I enjoy being with you. You're, well—"

I cut him off, feeling a bit embarrassed by the direction of his stuttering compliments. "Thanks. I'll try to be a good guest."

***

Temple Emanuel reminded me of a plush theater—soft lighting and cushy chairs, not uncomfortable pine pews like most churches. Leo said it was a reform temple, the liberal end of Judaism, but the sense of history, the rituals performed for millennia, filled my bones. His two sons—Sam, whose thirteen-year-old, Jordan, was the bar mitzvah, and Ben, who'd had the drug problem—looked like younger versions of Leo. Jordan had the same intense blue eyes and bushy eyebrows as the other men in his family. And Leo—what a transformation. He looked handsome and sophisticated in his dark gray suit and light blue shirt. I realized I'd never seen him in clothes before—except yoga pants and bathing suits, of course. The whole family was on the *bimah* and Leo's curly silver hair, his bald spot covered by his yarmulke, gleamed in the lights as he stood next to his family. His grandson's face was blotched red from nerves, although he had done a super job reading in Hebrew from the Torah. I knew their hearts were full of *nachas* as they all smiled for the cameras. Hot tears threatened my mascara while watching the love-fest.

I'd felt like an outsider from the moment we entered—I was one—but his sons and Sam's wife greeted me with hugs and everyone laughed when Jordan said, "Grandpa has a pretty girlfriend!" And Leo was treating me like his girlfriend, with his arm around my waist as he guided me down the aisle to sit up front. Lots of eyes followed us from around the room—I whispered to him that I felt like Lady Gaga. Leo leaned over and whispered back, "They're all jealous of my blonde *shiksa*."

Later we arrived at the top floor ballroom of a ritzy hotel for the party. His grandson loved baseball, so they'd hired perky young people wearing sexy Miami Marlins uniforms and referee outfits to greet us and wait on us. I was seated for dinner at the head table, still feeling like the odd person out while listening to many family in-jokes, which Leo tried to explain in hurried whispers. Course after course overwhelmed me—I felt like a French goose.

After dinner the "Hava Nagila" started playing and Leo grabbed me by the hand and dragged me, protesting, to the dance floor for the *hora*.

"I can't do this!" I shouted over the music.

"You said you're part Jewish, so prove it." Everyone at the tables clapped as two circles formed. I was soon jumping and kicking to the music, Leo's hand gripping mine, and a teenage boy holding me on the other side. The music kept going faster and faster, forcing more and more folks to drop out. Leo and I were the last seniors standing, dancing until I could no longer breathe and my makeup seemed in danger of melting.

As we staggered away from the dance floor, Leo looked at me and laughed.

"What?" I gasped out.

He gave me a quick hug. "You're great. And you're redder than Jordan after his speech!"

The rest of the evening continued the aerobic workout—jitterbug, twist, cha-cha interspersed with hip-hop. Leo continued nonstop, even trying the hip-hop: the Energizer Bunny! We danced and laughed. He was right—the party had lifted my veil of woe, and I felt like the homecoming queen. Four glasses of wine may have contributed to my coronation.

Toward the end of the party, a slow number finally started up. Leo led me out to the dance floor. I was sure I had BO by that time and I had removed the jacket to my dress long ago, exposing more cleavage than a woman my age should display. I'd almost had a wardrobe malfunction while doing the twist. By that point, Leo and most of the men who danced had dumped their ties and suit jackets. Leo held me so close I was afraid my Spanx might pop apart. The artful placement and pressure of his hand on my lower back pulled my midsection right onto his.

The closeness of his body to mine transported me back to a high school dance and my sexual awakening to Johnny Mathis's "crotch music" as Tony Martino made me feel his arousal by moving his hand lower and lower on my back and thrusting his erection against my stomach. Yes, I was getting hits from my erogenous zones again. But, no, I did not want to become sexually involved with Leo. He was seventy-five! Why did old people still want to couple? We should be planning our exits, not our weddings. However, even gripped by those gloomy thoughts, I was swooning just a little in his arms. He was a few inches taller than me and our bodies did seem to fit each other's perfectly.

As I staggered off the dance floor, a bit intoxicated and not just from the alcohol, the family, thankfully, was saying goodbyes. Lots of hugs and tears and another good line from his grandson: "Grandpa, we want you to bring your girlfriend tomorrow for breakfast. Mom's cooking for everyone."

Leo held my hand and whistled while we waited for the valet to get his car. Snuggled into his Lexus, we drove to our complex with George Winston's music playing—I leaned back and almost fell asleep! He helped me out of the car, took my hand, and guided me toward my elevator.

"No need for you to come up. I'll be fine," I told him.

He looked at me in the dim light and said, "Well. I've gotta ask—how about some friendly sex tonight?"

"As opposed to some *unfriendly* sex?" Both of us a wee bit tipsy, we laughed till we bent over, holding our stomachs.

"Yeah. And I know—I shouldn't have asked! Not with all the pressure you're under. But I'm falling for you, you must know that by now!"

"Hmm, yeah, I'm just not ready to…not until…but, I had a great time tonight—you were right about the party taking my mind off Alyssa. And I love your family, especially your *mensch* of a grandson."

"I'd like to pick you up tomorrow at nine for the biggest breakfast you'll ever see. I need to keep 'my girlfriend' or Jordan will be disappointed in me. Okay?"

"Sure. I'd love to go."

The elevator door opened and he stepped in right behind me. "I'm making sure you get in safely—Quinton and all—so don't argue." As we started up, Leo gathered me up in his arms for a long, lingering kiss. He was good! I did not resist and let myself enjoy the feeling of two tired bodies humming together. But at my door, I said a firm, "Good night."

Chapter 13

It had rained earlier that morning and the air was clean and clear. The sun was shining in on my porch as I sipped a cup of coffee before going downstairs to meet Leo for the post-bar mitzvah breakfast. I'd had a wonderful time at the party; I'd danced more in one evening than in the past eight or nine years combined, so it was a two-Aleve morning for my sore feet and ankles. Cute, strappy sandals—we used to call them "fuck-me" shoes—were not meant for sixty-nine-year-old gals. But wow, for seventy-five, Leo was in amazing shape. He'd outlasted me and still had enough post-party energy to ask for sex! He certainly was direct. Although I liked him, and his family too, I was not going to let our relationship move quickly into a sticky affair. If we started something and it bombed, I wouldn't feel comfortable at the pool or at my yoga classes with an ex-boyfriend next to me. *Boyfriend.* What a term for a senior citizen's seventy-five-year-old *squeeze*. We needed new terminology for all the old farts going at dating with the help of the oodles of new websites. Maybe "oldie with benefits" or my "crone-friend." A few years ago, we mature adults would have been advised to take up golf or gardening and retire from the opposite sex. Probably the little blue pill contributed to the rush to couple as much as the Internet did.

Back in Leo's Lexus, the lingering dampness made everything green glitter in the sunshine. Leo said, "Gorgeous out today. Would you like the top down? I don't want to mess up your hair."

"I'd love to feel the wind." I looked up at the hard roof. "Doesn't look like this is a convertible, though."

His gleeful smile revealed how much he loved showing off his car. He stopped on the roadside and pushed a button—the hard top automatically folded itself into the trunk. What amazing engineering. I was about thirty the last time I sped along with a top down. *Yahoo*!

"You okay, Maureen?"

"Couldn't be better."

Leo started with the throat noises again, then said, "My ex-wife would've never let me put the top down. Mess up her thousand-dollar hairdo? Never. Sorry, poisonous topic."

"I wondered if I'd meet her at the bar mitzvah last night."

"She lives in London—on me—and had some excuse why she couldn't come for her grandson's big day. My son—our son—will never forgive her."

"I'm sorry, for Jordan's sake especially."

"She was never close to her own children and has no interest in her two grandchildren. I would never have stayed married for twenty years except I knew my boys needed me."

"I'm sorry, I—"

"It was like being married to an evil castrating chicken."

I choked. "A what?"

"Whenever she'd see a weak spot in my psyche, she'd peck away at it until I bled. It took me years to feel happy again." He glanced over at me. "I'm sorry I unloaded on you."

"You've got to feel proud of your children. And Jordan—my new boyfriend."

"He really took to you. He's got good taste. He even called me this morning to make sure you were coming."

We pulled into the circular drive of a lovely two-story Mediterranean-style house and walked up the front path. Jordan opened the door as we climbed the front stairs. He hugged his grandfather and said shyly, glancing down, "Hi, Maureen. I'm glad you came."

We stepped inside where about twenty people were already loading plates from the dining room table: bagels, whitefish, cream cheese, lox, chocolate babka, and much more. It reminded me of the many buffets at Susan's mother's home in Queens during our college years, when her family would all try to fatten me up. Jordan's parents, Sam and Marion, came over and hugged both of us. They acted as though Leo and I were getting married soon. Leo's sister, Bea, a large buxom woman with big hair, said in a bold voice, "You ever heard of the play *Abie's Irish Rose?*" I had not. "It's about a Jewish guy who marries an Irish Catholic girl."

Leo said, "About a very young Jewish guy in 1922."

After being reintroduced to a few more guests, we loaded up our plates and sat next to Jordan and his younger brother on the lanai. As soon as I finished eating and laid my fork down, Jordan jumped up. "Can I show you my room now, Maureen?"

Leo gave him a nudge and said, "Stealing my girlfriend already, Jordy? Maybe she's still hungry."

I laughed, got up, and followed Jordan up the wide staircase to his room. What a young man cave! Computer center, drum set, electric upright bass, shelves full of trophies and books, posters of baseball greats, an autographed baseball in a case.

"Wow, Jordan. This is awesome. You play drums and bass?"

"Yeah. Mostly drums."

"And your trophies—they're all for baseball? I figured you loved it after seeing the costumes last night."

"I'm pretty good. I hope I get a scholarship to play in college. Can you come to one of my games? I pitch."

"Sure."

"Wanna see the YouTube video me and my friend made?"

Leo stepped in and said, "I'm taking her back. I want her to meet someone."

We went downstairs and Leo introduced me to a few others, always with pride in his voice, as though I was his fiancée. Later, when Sam, Marion, and Jordan walked us to the car, Jordan asked Leo to bring me to his game Tuesday night. I was getting a little nervous about expectations on Leo's part and his family's.

On the way home, Leo told me his family liked me and Jordan wanted to adopt me as his grandma. Jordan's maternal grandmother had died very young and he had no relationship with Leo's ex. It saddened me to think that my relationship with Jordy might be as close as I would get to becoming a grandmother.

***

I had not seen love-struck Susan in a few days—she and Michael were spending so much time together they were going to OD. Was I jealous? I didn't think so, but I felt like I'd lost a part of me. Maybe my estrangement from my own sister, and now Sue's dumping me for Michael...*oh, stop the stupid thoughts. Shut them down.*

After yoga, I drove to the café, picked up my coffee and scone, and joined Susan at *our* table, although it was becoming Leo's and my table also.

"Hi, Sue. I've missed you. What's new?"

Sue laughed. "Is this a rhyming day, Reenie?"

My friends, family, and all my students knew me as the serial rhymer. I did it subconsciously—a little too often.

"How was the bar mitzvah with Leo?"

"I had a blast—a great tension reliever. And Leo—I was so wrong. He's not Leo the Lecher, he's Leo the Lionhearted."

Susan grinned. "So we both got old geezer boyfriends."

"Yours appears to be a lot more serious, if you measure number of hours together. Have you moved in with him yet?"

"Hey. We spend every night home—alone. No sex. I don't think either one of us is capable."

"So, he hasn't smooched or groped or—"

"Well. We went on a sunset cruise last night, had a few cocktails on board. We rarely drink that much. Then we sat in a dark corner on the deck coming home—one of his arms was around my back, the other, kinda short his arms, tried to wrap around my big boobs and he smooched away. Two old fatsos—embarrassing. He ended up sort of holding on my right one 'cause he couldn't reach around them. Ha! Well, maybe he could've reached."

"What a picture." We both hooted and again our table attracted an audience. Showtime.

We talked until Sue stood up and did a little pirouette. "So—you noticin' yet?"

"Yeah. You look fantastic. New body. New clothes. New boyfriend. I love you, Sue."

"And I love you too."

When I left, I no longer felt abandoned.

Chapter 14

Tuesday evening I met Leo in the courtyard to go to Jordan's baseball game. Jordy's school was set to play their archrival. I was feeling sucked into his family—a good, warm sucking, though.

I agreed to have the top down again and we sped off down a long stretch of highway. I closed my eyes and we were flying. I was disappointed when we landed in a middle school lot. We'd planned a late arrival so we wouldn't have to sit through the entire game. Leo brought two canvas chairs and we perched next to the bleachers. Jordan spotted us from the dugout and waved. He looked adorable in his baseball uniform, his curly dark hair peeking out around his hat. His father waved from the second row.

A minute later, Jordan was up at bat. I'd always felt too much empathy for any child at bat—such pressure on a young person. I usually closed my eyes until it was over, but Jordan's bat connected with the first pitch, a hard drive toward third base, and he made it to first with time to spare, giving us a little thumbs-up. We spent the next hour cheering for his team. I was transported into a new world.

When the game ended and we'd said our goodbyes and congrats, I knew I was just a little in love—with Leo, or maybe with this warm family?

"A drink at the Seaside Bar before home or, better yet, my bar?"

"Hmm. I think the Seaside sounds safer. Your bar sounds too much like it might have 'friendly sex' attached."

The Seaside's lounge was almost empty on a Tuesday evening, and its bare bar was depressing. Leo looked at me and said, "My home is much cozier than this. I won't attack you—promise." He gave me the old Boy Scout three-finger salute.

I'd never seen Leo's apartment before. Since it was on the ground floor, his lanai opened onto a lovely outside garden with a little fountain burbling, and just past there, a mini-lake. (In Florida, anything larger than a mud puddle is called a lake.) His living room had sleek black leather sofas and an Eames lounge chair. Glass and stainless steel tables gleamed in the lamplight, while colorful abstract art covered his walls—the black furniture set off the paintings. A bouquet of freesia perfumed the room. I'd always been mesmerized by that sweet scent.

"Please. Sit. I've got limoncello in the freezer, a good cold Sauvignon Blanc, and—"

"Limoncello, please. I love it."

He brought over two drinks in elegant stemmed glasses and sat next to me on the soft black leather. "I should put on some Johnny Mathis—a little mood music?" He had a cockeyed grin on his face and I knew he was joking.

"Oh, no. Not Mathis. Not fair."

He laughed. "Well. Cheers." We clunked glasses and sipped the tart, sweet drink. "I know you taught college. I'll bet you were a great teacher."

"I was good." I had to smile—I had been highly rated by ninety-five percent of my students. "That sounds self-serving, but my older career-changing students, who appreciated honesty and good teaching, sang my praises—and I gave them personal attention. A few of the eighteen-year-old guys—I called those the nose-pickers—dropped my classes when they found out they had to work. But I am a ham, so teaching was also my stage."

We discussed our careers. I was in awe of physicians and it sounded like Leo was a truly compassionate doc. He said, "I discovered early on a doctor has to spend the extra few minutes it takes to form a bond with each patient if you expect them to tell you all their symptoms. I gave my chronically ill patients little pocket diaries to record things they wanted to tell me. Most patients brought their diaries to each visit. And I had my receptionist call my needy patients to remind them to exercise and eat right and refill their prescriptions."

Leo's arm slipped around me as he talked, and he pulled me close, snuggling his head into my neck. "I want you to be part of my life, Maureen. But I don't want to scare you away—can I just hold you?"

My life had become a soap opera. There I was on a sofa in another man's apartment not two weeks after my accidental sofa-sex with Bob. Weird coincidences: they were both Jews, and one was "silver" and the other "gold." More life had happened to me in the past three weeks than in the past two years.

We stayed nestled together quietly for several minutes, his hand rhythmically rubbing my upper arm, lulling me into a semi-conscious state. When his arm-rubbing shifted to left-nipple-rubbing and I felt my motor starting, I pushed him off. "You promised, Leo."

"Just testing your resolve. I'll wait—as long as it takes. But I better get you home 'cause I want to touch every part of you."

I thought only younger men were so charged. I knocked down the rest of my drink. Leo was soon holding my hand as we made our way back to my front door. I was glad we didn't run into Bob, although I had a suspicion Bob was taking the stairs every day to avoid meeting me. As I turned my key in my lock, Leo hugged me from behind and whispered, "Good night, my Irish rose."

***

The next morning I was stuffing down my oatmeal, camouflaged by lots of brown sugar, and was planning a good sit-down talk with myself when the phone rang. I listened for its computer voice and heard "unknown caller." I grabbed it in case it was Alyssa and heard Quinton's strong voice. "Maureen. I found her. She's back with that old bastard she lived with before."

I fell into a chair, hope and fear boxing in my head. "Did you talk to her?" I think I shouted into the phone.

"I reached this Darius guy on his cell but he won't let me talk to Alyssa. Got their address, though, and I heard from a pretty good source that they're both shooting up now—it's bad."

At first, I was speechless. He could have been wrong; people do spread rumors. My twittering mind said Alyssa could not have sunk so low. I said, "Tell me how bad."

After I insisted, Quinton told me my worst nightmares were true—she was shooting up heroin, and he'd heard she was selling her body to pay for it. A huge pain filled my head and I screamed, "Nooo," but maybe the scream was just inside my skull. The phone was on the floor; I couldn't remember if the call was over.

I staggered over to the counter to hold on, overwhelmed by nausea. My mouth barely made it to the kitchen sink where I vomited my oatmeal. Gasping and gagging, I heaved up everything, almost choking to death on my own puke.

When I could breathe and stand again, I got a glass of club soda and started taking little sips, hoping it would clear out my throat and mouth. I decided to call Sean to get some help, although he was obviously not as good a private eye as Quinton. I caught him in his car doing surveillance. My voice was feeble, like my mother's just before she died, but Sean did most of the talking.

On speakerphone, Sean's sharp Brooklyn-accented voice filled my kitchen. "This is what I think ya need to do. I know a good interventionist here you can hire. He'll help you plan everything. His name is Jake Rogers; he's got a great team of folks and he has personal connections with quite a few rehab facilities. Can you afford to send Alyssa to rehab? It might cost twenty-five or thirty grand a month, and she'll need a few months, I think."

Luckily, I could swing the cost since John and I had sold several properties in New Jersey before the economy collapsed. As a contractor, John had many investment opportunities, and his acumen at knowing when to buy and sell could be what saved his daughter. Alyssa had truly loved her dad and his construction work—I wanted her to know that her dad was still helping her.

Sean continued his rapid-fire orders: "Jake, he'll work with ya and set everything up, and I'll get Quinton to help get her to the intervention. This might take a while, and you'll have to be on standby and ready to get your group to New York with maybe only a day's notice. The goal of the intervention is to get her to agree right then and there to get in a car and go to the facility."

Of course I told Sean I could do all that, but in actuality I could not even stand up. Did I want to work with two New York strangers? Did I really need them? My logic was overwhelmed by my emotions—yet again. So much horrifying stuff to do, and so quickly. Who to call? I had only one close relative, my sister, and we hadn't spoken since John's funeral. Susan was more of an aunt to Alyssa than Tara. I immediately knew I wanted, needed, Leo with me, but he barely knew Alyssa. Would he come? What a test of his friendship. Would Susan take time off from Michael? Was it too much to ask her to come to New York City and confront Alyssa? An intervention would certainly scorch everyone involved. Clear thinking was impossible and my panicked thoughts could lead to bad decisions; I knew this. I put on some jazzed-up Bach, covered my eyes with a cold cloth, and lay down on the sofa before I fell over— no Valium, not yet. I needed my mind to work, not hide out.

A few minutes later, I felt my heart revving up to a terrifying speed—it was jumping, thumping about, like the monster from *Alien* trying to be born—and I could not breathe. I tried to sit up but the pounding in my chest made me dizzy and faint. I reached my cell, held the button down, and told it to call Leo. Thankfully he answered. "Leo, help, my heart…"

"Just hang up. I'm calling 911 and I'm coming up."

I didn't fully pass out, but my breathing was not bringing in oxygen and I was ready to give in—it would be a relief, an excuse to escape. Blackness floated over me when Susan's voice brought me back; Leo must have roused her to get her key to my place. I could hear Leo's voice until my goddamn shrieking alarm system went off.

Susan was standing over me. "What's your alarm code?"

I could barely croak it out.

Leo said, "Just follow doctor's orders, okay?" then he held a paper bag over my face and told me to breathe slowly. That helped a little. My consciousness was rotating on the ceiling fan, looking down on my bagged body. I rejoined my corporeal self when I felt Leo's cold stethoscope moving around my chest. Then his fingers were on my neck, taking my pulse and telling me to relax. *Yeah, sure.*

With a lot of noise and clanking, two young men who spoke in crisp medical terms wheeled in a gurney. The rest was a blur of fear— I was strapped onto a gurney for the first time in my life. I had to be sitting up to get down the elevator. Then I was flat out in the back of the ambulance—sirens wailing! Leo was holding my hand; a technician was taking all my vitals and sending them ahead to the hospital. I kept trying to talk, but there was an oxygen mask over my face so only gibberish came out. The stink of ammonia seeped under my mask and made me feel nauseated again. I bolted up, pulling off the mask, gagging, ready to vomit.

Leo held me. "You're gonna be fine, sweetheart." He tried to smile, but he looked too frightened to be a comfort. "Has your heart ever raced like this before?" His voice warmed my ear as he eased me back down.

I lifted the mask again to answer, "Yes. A couple of times when John was dying in hospice. But never this badly." My usual snappy speaking voice had become a baby bird voice—each word peeped out.

I was relieved Leo was with me in the emergency room's roomette, that very non-private curtained-off place where they hook you up to all the monitors and treat you like a piece of numbered meat. The doctor on duty knew him, and I guess I was getting VIP service. Leo stepped out of my curtained area and, *oh shit*, Bob stepped in. I must have looked horrified at the thought of Bob doing nurse duty on me.

He must have noticed my repulsion. "Relax, I'm not your ER nurse, but I'm glad to see Leo is getting you taken care of quickly. Have someone page me if you want to talk." Then he was rubbing my IVed hand, which was icy cold. "I'm fixing this IV so your hand's not so cold."

My circuits were all overloaded, but I knew I had to get strong—I had a daughter to save.

Thankfully, I didn't have to spend the night in the hospital. Susan picked Leo and me up and I sat next to her while Leo rubbed my shoulders from the back seat. The ER doc had given me an anti-anxiety medication after he was sure I was having an acute panic attack, not a heart attack. I was still feeling a little woozy.

Leo, in his new bossy-doctor voice, said, "You're not staying alone tonight! If Susan can't stay, I will." His doctor persona allowed no disagreement. Susan said she would stay with me and gave my arm a squeeze. They both knew the short version of the Alyssa-Sean-Quinton story, which had probably brought on my "attack." Three subdued and quiet people made the thirty-minute ride home. Leo kept up his relaxing massage. Unfortunately, I caught a glimpse of myself in the rearview mirror and saw a sagging, old woman's face— *not me, couldn't be me.* I glanced around at Leo and Susan and they looked haggard also. We were too old for that much trauma and worry.

By the time they'd settled me back home on my sofa it was dinnertime, and Leo insisted we bring in Chinese food and all eat something. I just wanted to sleep, but Leo, in doctor mode, ordered food and told me I had to eat. I staggered into the bathroom to do a few repairs to improve my hag-look and then was almost force-fed by

Leo. After getting down a little ginger chicken and some lo mein, my face fell forward and Susan hustled Leo out.

She helped me into pajamas and propped me up in my bed. "I'm gonna read to you and you're not answering any phone calls or emails tonight." Susan, who hates poetry, read from, of all my books, Garrison Keillor's *Good Poems*. I was asleep by the third poem massacred by Sue's still-vital Queens accent.

***

The next day Sue served me rubber eggs and burned toast—I hoped her boyfriend Michael wasn't looking for a cook. I shooed her out after breakfast, assuring her I was fine. I felt some of my old mental strength returning—time to talk to Mr. Rogers, gather my intervention team, and stop wallowing in a cocoon of self-pity. I'd blocked off the ability to feel joy since the day John's doctor gave us his death sentence. I was unable to appreciate the six years we had together after his diagnosis, and my hyper-vigilance drove us both crazy at times.

I remembered yelling at him, too often, "You forgot to take your meds this morning. I checked your holder."

"Stop spying on me. I'll get to them when my stomach feels less queasy. Yesterday, I puked them up."

"I should call Dr. Drummond. Maybe he'll prescribe some anti-nausea med. Okay, hon?"

"Just let me deal with it, Maureen. I love ya, but it's my body."

Since his death, I'd gone permanently off the rails of happiness. I gave in to misery, wallowed in it—it was easier than fighting it.

I was determined to prove FA wrong. I would not "release with love," would not be powerless, and would not give in to a "higher power." I called Jake Rogers, the interventionist (why did I think the *illusionist*?), after I'd spent a few hours on the Internet studying that new career path and reading about Jake's company, Rogers' Mediation Services. Interventionists apparently did not believe in FA's philosophy either, but you had to have money to get involved with them. Or damn good insurance.

When he called me back, I said, "I hope it's okay to call you Jake, 'cause I refuse to call you Mr. Rogers." My silly-assed opening.

"Then I'll call you Maureen, not Mrs. Manning. I spoke to Sean earlier and he briefed me with what he knows. I'd like you to tell me all you can about Alyssa and, if it's okay with you, I'll ask Quinton to do the same. This is so I can choose the best rehab for her." His voice was strong and had a warm and reassuring quality—or was that just my wishful thinking? All I managed was grunts in response as he spoke.

"This'll take about a week—to get everything set up and to rehearse with Alyssa's friends and relatives. I'll email you a contract and we'll get right to work. And paying for rehab is doable? Right?"

I assured Jake I could pay and asked if Alyssa could rehab somewhere in Florida where I could visit. I knew some world-class rehab places were right near me.

"The facilities I know well are all in New York, Jersey, Pennsylvania, and Vermont and, ideally, we want to be able to put her in a car going straight out to her rehab. And there's limited visiting, especially the first month."

After listening to Jake I could not think—a garbage disposal in my brain kept grinding up my synapses. I made a yogurt smoothie, the only food that might slide down, and sat on my porch. I needed a rest before more stressful phoning. As soon as I got my feet up, my cell rang—Doctor Leo.

"Maureen, how are you feeling today?"

"Fine, Doctor. Strong. Ready for battle!"

"I want to be with you for this battle—just call me your private physician. I don't want you going to New York, or anywhere, without me. Okay?"

"Wow. You saved me from begging. I want you to be part of the intervention we're planning. It'll be soon, probably in Brooklyn. Will you come to that too?"

"I won't leave your side. And I've got a friend with an apartment in Manhattan he rarely uses. I'll set it up for you and, I'm betting, Susan. I'll stay with a cousin in Queens."

"Thank you. That's a big help. I'd hate to be in a hotel room waiting for this."

"And I'm taking you to a special yoga class tomorrow—don't say no; you need some relaxing physical exercise, that's doctor's orders. You can't sit there alone and worry."

***

Well, I had Quinton, Susan, and Leo on my team, and of course Jake Rogers would be there. It sounded a bit meager. Quinton was going to ask Alyssa's college roommate, Jenny Wu, to come. She lived in Boston and had become a well-known tattoo artist. I could not picture tiny Jenny Wu tattooing muscled Hells Angels, but half the young people I'd met recently had at least one tattoo showing, my daughter included. I'd spied a colorful butterfly on her lower back when she came back from the pool.

I decided against calling my sister, but I emailed her the whole Alyssa story and asked her to call me if she could take time off from her law firm and come to the intervention. If she called and asked to come, that would be a breakthrough. Tara lived in Philly and was five years younger than I, three times divorced, and childless. She had been close to my daughter, but only prior to Alyssa's teen years. For the past two years, she'd refused to speak to me because I'd said something at John's funeral that upset her.

Afterwards I had to wait for Sean or Jake to call me: two men I'd never met in person who had my daughter's life in their hands. I was living inside a nightmare—everything was surreal. Sean and Jake had set up a Skype session with me for the next day, so at least I'd see their faces. I went back to my friend, Google, to learn more about interventions. Quite complicated, I slowly learned. After several more hours of study, I discovered actual addicts' interventions I could watch on YouTube. There were conflicting opinions on the outcomes, but most were hopeful. My team would be coached to write "letters" we would take turns reading to Alyssa, the purpose to motivate her to accept immediate treatment.

What did less-affluent people do, who didn't have family who could afford interventionists and expensive rehab? I tried not to obsess when reading about young people who had been through multiple relapses and rehabs. Wasn't Alyssa smarter than most, more talented? Didn't she have more to live for than some of the case studies I read?

Chapter 15

Leo was right. The restorative yoga class was therapeutic—all the kinks from laying around in the hospital and all the stress, from everything, were being gently pushed out of me through long, supported poses. Leo was on my right side and studying my every move, giving me a little smile whenever he caught my eye. After the ninety minutes were over, I felt emotionally refreshed—I was breathing deeply again, not those shallow, unhealthy breaths. We had a quick breakfast together since I had many phone calls to make. If I'd allowed him, I think Leo would have moved into my condo to hover over me day and night—a guardian angel. I loved his support, but I'd always needed alone time and privacy, and it looked like Leo wanted just the opposite. When he dropped me off he asked, "When will I see you again?"

Oy! "Not today. I've got phone calls, emails, and Skyping to do...then I think I'll watch *Doc Martin* reruns before bed."

"Call me if you need anything! Promise? And who is Doc Martin?"

"A hilarious British comedy about a physician who has Asperger's."

"I love Britcoms. I'll try it out tonight. And let me make you dinner on Saturday. I barbeque a mean steak and a little red meat is good for you. Same promise goes, okay?"

I agreed to Saturday's dinner and hightailed it back to my place. Emails bleeped in when I opened my computer. Quinton's missive said Jenny, Alyssa's former roommate, would come down from Boston by train for the intervention—she could leave her tattoo business anytime. My sister, Tara, emailed she would come "if needed." What the hell did that mean? Call and beg if I wanted her there? I did not have time to beg. I had emailed Sylvia the short version of recent events and she'd replied, "I wish you and Alyssa the best possible intervention outcome. Call me. See you at church on Sunday, maybe?"

After lunch, I put my MacBook high on my desk so the camera would line up with my face and sat waiting for Jake to initiate the call that would also include Sean. I soon heard the odd little Skype ring and quickly answered. Jake began. He was wearing a jacket and tie, not something I saw often around the Gardens, and he had a commanding voice—I knew he was an ex-narcotics detective who had earned a degree in counseling. He set out the next steps for our team. He would email me samples of the confrontational letters that each member of my team would have to compose immediately. We would then send our drafts to him for review. There was no time for a rehearsal, but he would Skype with a larger group later if needed.

"I'm going under the assumption that Quinton's and Sean's investigations are true, so we need to move fast. Your daughter is in great danger if she's prostituting herself."

Those words—I still could not believe they were true.

Sean answered. He had gray, wavy hair, lots of it, and was dressed in a black T-shirt. "I've checked things out and she is living with this Darius guy. He's a known user and, I'm betting, also a small-time dealer—most need to deal to pay for their own habit. I think she's past the stage where we can just invite her to join us, but I'll figure out a way to get her to our meeting."

I decided I'd never again Skype for a pleasurable conversation after we shut down the agonizing session. "Prostituting herself" still echoed with the reverberations of an assault rifle firing in my brain—I wished I could shut that down with a click. Darius was the one who threw her out of his apartment a couple of years ago, the one I called Shithead. He went to Pratt too, and was an artist, I remembered. And Alyssa was devastated when he threw her out. My heartbeat felt like a fast jazz riff.

After lunch, Jake emailed his instructions and I forwarded them to Quinton and Susan. Jake's email said he'd found an opening at a "wonderful rehab" in northern Vermont—wasn't that an oxymoron. He gave permission for Leo to come as my physician and, since Leo did not know Alyssa well enough to confront her, he could tell the happy-ending story about his son's rehab. Jake thought I should read my letter first, Quinton second, and, if we were lucky, perhaps that would be enough for her to agree to rehab. He'd said during our

Skype session, "Since Alyssa obviously tried to get help by showing up at your apartment, I believe she must want to change her life."

Later, I sat at my computer and tried to follow Jake's admonitions on intervention letters. It took all my mental strength to write it—tears dripping onto my computer as I typed each word. Part of me still did not believe any of it was happening—Alyssa would just show up at the door with her iPhone in one hand, her computer in the other…

Alyssa, my dear daughter,

I am here today because I love and care about you. I want you to be safe and healthy. That's why I want you to get treatment for your drug abuse.

I remember you coming to work with me when you were in grade school and sitting next to me at my desk. You had zillions of questions—I only wish some of my students had been as smart and interested as you were as a child. Remember when we played computer games together and you always won? I knew you would become a computer maven.

Your dad thought you were the most beautiful, the most intelligent, and the most amazing girl. He loved skiing with you even though you beat him down the slopes. We both loved playing tennis with you. All of us had fun going to Long Beach Island in the summers. Remember when my bathing suit bottom got pulled down by a big wave and the fishermen clapped?

We were both so proud of your scholarship to Pratt and your amazing talents as an artist and an animator. I've been bragging about you to all my friends since you were born.

Now I am consumed by worry. You told me you have lost jobs, lost apartments, and I know you have borrowed twenty-thousand dollars from me over the past few years.

I know your health is suffering by looking at your skin and your hair and hearing your ragged voice and seeing how thin you are.

I have been terribly worried about you ever since you came to my home just a month ago looking so sick. When I learned about your addictions, I got physically ill. My migraines have come back and sometimes I can't keep food down. I was sent to the ER last week with what seemed like a heart attack. I could not breathe. All because I am worried about my beautiful daughter.

I am on medication now so I don't have another anxiety or panic attack. I am afraid to answer the phone because of my fears about your health and safety.

I am afraid you will die of an overdose if you don't get extensive help immediately. With the help of Jake Rogers, I have made arrangements for you to go to a rehab in Vermont that specializes in helping people with addictions and co-occurring disorders like bipolar. Also, many artists and creative people go to this rehab. It's a beautiful place in the mountains and will remind you of our family trips to Jay Peak to ski.

We can drive you straight to Vermont right after this meeting and send on anything you might need. Are you willing to go for treatment, right now, to be healthy and safe again?

I am here out of love for you. I know this is harsh and difficult for you, and it is for me too. I hope I was a good mother in the past, but I know this is the most loving thing I've ever done for you.

I could not complete the end of the letter—the part where I'd been instructed to tell her what I would do as consequences if she refused treatment. After I emailed Jake my epistle, Susan sent me a copy of her letter to Alyssa and I cried as I read it. Hers was laced with Yiddish hyperbole, but it was from her heart and must have pained her to write it.

My brain craved escape from my apocalyptic life, so I started watching, for the second time, *The Forsyte Saga*, a depressing but compelling British period drama. Curled up with a truly decadent bowl of Ben & Jerry's Coffee Toffee Bar Crunch, I lost myself in the 1800s until I fell asleep hours later, the melodramas of the Victorian era mixing with my own life's drama in a gibberish-sugar-dream stew. I woke with a furry mouth, a smelly body, and an ice cream hangover, and transferred my disgusting bod to bed.

***

The next morning I went into a cleaning frenzy, always a good way to avoid too much thinking. Except for the mess in Alyssa's room, I polished, scrubbed, and laundered until I was lathered, then went to work on my hair and body—my BO had become a chemical weapon. When I was as sparkly as my home, I ate a light lunch and considered my dinner date that night. I had just told Susan that at our age a romance could not move too quickly, but I was uncomfortable with Leo's fast pace. Perhaps if my life was not in such a free-fall, I might not be putting on the brakes so often. I would have to be honest with Leo, though—I did not want to share my bed or bathroom with any man, or any human, ever again. I really did not even want to have dinner with him, but I knew the depression I was already feeling would only worsen if I sat at home alone. It was a testament to his caring that he wanted to spend time with me at all. Lots of jolly widows mined the pool each day for the few free men, some with boobs prominently displayed and reddened lips pouting at each man still able to walk.

Even depressed, I put on my face and dressed in a long, white gauzy skirt and yet another blue T-shirt. I rang Leo's doorbell at seven sharp. When he opened the door, I admired his blue Hawaiian-style shirt. His blue eyes gleamed, and the shirt camouflaged his post-middle-age belly. He looked fit and tan in white Bermuda shorts and sandals. Why did most men his age have legs in better shape than mine?

"It's a pleasure to see a beautiful woman at my door. Come in."

I paused on the threshold a moment, then stepped into his unavoidable open arms and a warm hug.

He broke off as he asked, "I've got gin and tonic, red or white wine, and iced tea. What'll it be?"

"G&T please. Strong! Can I help?"

"Just go out to the lanai and I'll bring drinks."

We sat across from each other on deep-cushioned wicker chairs, the sliders all open to a lovely breeze bringing in the scent of the night-blooming jasmine from his patio.

"I was going to get out my stethoscope and check you out, but you look healthy tonight."

"And I just might have questioned your motives for listening to my heart."

We both laughed and sipped our drinks. Huge, billowy clouds scuttled around the setting sun, turning the sky pink and purple. My ears picked up tinkle-music, probably Mozart, playing softly from his stereo. A giant heron and an egret were walking along the edge of the pond-lake several yards from his patio. Watching water and birds always relaxed me, and judging from the price of waterfront property, it must do so for most humans.

We were quiet for an almost uncomfortable time. Finally, Leo said, "I don't want to awaken the elephant in the room, or maybe a herd of them, so you're the leader tonight."

"Don't worry. I'm okay. And you volunteered to come to the intervention, so feel free to talk about anything. We seem to be in this together."

"In this together—hearing you say that makes me very happy." He gave me his Joe Biden smile. "Now I'll grill the steak and you can dress the salad and put it out."

I could not do justice to Leo's lovely dinner. His London broil was delicious and his potatoes from the grill were yummy with garlic and onions, but great food and great company only made me think more about Alyssa's pathetic life.

Leo was working to keep the conversation upbeat, while my mind was trying hard just to stay sane. "Leo, I'm sorry I'm such an awful guest tonight. My brain is unable to 'live in the moment,' as Anika often tells us, hard as I try."

"I figured you'd be down, so I've got a treat for you, for us, right after I throw these dishes into the kitchen and get us each a limoncello." He efficiently cleared the table, then walked me over to the sofa facing a wall with a huge built-in TV. He handed me my drink and started juggling his three remotes. "I watched the first episode of *Doc Martin* last night. You were right—I love it. I thought we'd watch episode two together."

The music introducing the show refocused my brain, and the views of the charming little seaside village in England lifted my spirits. Soon we were laughing at Doc Martin's antics and snuggling together on the sofa like teenagers at the movies. By the end of the show I said, "Good medicine, Dr. Leo. I feel much better...but I should go now."

"Please stay." He was wrapped around me and his words were spoken directly into my ear. "I'd like to just hold you for a while, okay?"

"Can I say something first?

"Wait. Let me say...I'm falling in love with you, Maureen. I want you to be part of the rest of my life—in every way. To laugh with, cry with, to hold my hand when I'm dying—"

"Stop! Let me talk. I'm falling for you too, but...but I never want to sleep in the same bed, not even the same room, with anyone ever again. I don't want to share a bathroom or—"

"Okay, okay. That's a problem we can solve. I'm seventy-five but I'm healthy, and both my parents lived to be over ninety with all their marbles and, well, if we wait too long, we'll end up alone..."

Leo had tears in his blue eyes, which made them look huge. I held him close, feeling an uncomfortable déjà vu as he kissed my face and neck, then nibbled my lips. Without warning he slipped his hand under my T-shirt and began thumbing my nipple until the pulse between my legs matched his rhythm and my body unconsciously emitted a long moan.

I shoved him away. "I have to go. If it wasn't for...Alyssa and...then, I'd...maybe stay."

"I'm sorry. Broke that promise again, didn't I." He got up slowly and pulled me along. "I'll walk you back to your door," he said, his voice resigned, not angry.

We walked back in silence, his hand holding tightly to mine. I put my key in my door and turned toward Leo. "Sorry I can't relax and enjoy anything now. Thanks for putting up with me."

"Come here." He held me close, very close. That warm embrace, it ignited memories all the way back to my childhood. My father could cure the worst suffering—those painful insults all children receive—with his big bear embrace. Seventh grade was hell from beginning to end—I was flat-chested, the only one without her "monthly," and teased by everyone, including teachers, because I turned red-faced so quickly. Dad would come home and see my teary eyes and say, "Get over here, beautiful." He'd open his arms and I'd be enveloped in love.

Hugs are good medicine. Leo let me go after a few minutes and said, "Things will work out. You'll see."

Chapter 16

With great effort, I hauled myself to church on Sunday. The beautiful grounds and lovely sanctuary were a balm for my wounded psyche. Our minister gave an often-amusing sermon asking, "How old are you in your dreams?" A large number of our congregants were over seventy, many over eighty, and she made a game of having us remember our younger selves—when we were teens, newlyweds, or new parents—and how our former selves turn up when we close our eyes. Of course my faucets leaked a little while remembering John standing next to me at the altar, telling me I was the most beautiful bride, even though I knew my hairdresser had turned my hair into a concrete slab and the extra concealer barely covered a doozy of a nose zit.

On the patio after the service, four women from my spirituality group formed a corral around me. I told them about the upcoming intervention in New York and received plenty of hugs.

Sylvia said, "I'll go with you if you need support."

"No thanks, dear, I've got enough people coming with me."

Millie asked, "Do you want to come over for dinner tonight? My husband's away and we could talk."

Everyone wanted to help, but what could my friends do, really? What I needed was a way to cure my daughter, nothing else. I thought of my Roman Catholic upbringing—I always described myself as a "recovering" Catholic. What would a priest be telling me now? Just pray for help from Jesus. When I was in high school, I'd asked Father O'Malley, "Millions of good people are praying for world peace and we keep having wars; millions pray to God to heal their sick relatives and most still die. Good people pray for good things and bad things happen to them, so how can anyone believe in prayer?"

The bell saved him from answering, but he gave me a mean "I'll get you later" look.

***

I drove home in a trance state, with no memory of traffic, cars, or steering. I'd become a danger to myself and others. Walking toward the elevator, I squealed when I felt a tap on my shoulder. There was Bob, the man I used to go out of my way to meet. "Sorry I scared you, Maureen. Can you stop in for coffee? I need to talk to you."

His Richard Burton voice still sparked a little fire in my belly—I wanted to ask him why he hadn't taken the elevator in ages, but said, "Okay. I could use some caffeine." Another person jumped on the elevator with us, so we were silent. At his apartment, I sat at the kitchen counter and watched him start a smooth jazz album on the turntable, then prime the coffee pot.

Turning to me, he said, "Look, there's something I've wanted to say—well, explain—for a while now. And I'm not sure how to." He walked around the counter and sat down next to me. He had a strange grin on his face. Before I could say a word, he continued. "It's the age thing. I really like you, but, well, my mother was seventy-eight when she died, and..."

I couldn't hold back an uncomfortable giggle. Of course I knew how he felt about my age. He'd choked on his coffee when I told him. "I figured as much. But don't worry—you know I've been dating Leo for a while." I poked his arm. "And, actually, I felt you were a little too young for me."

"Well, Leo is a lucky guy. You're an attractive woman—and you do look young for—"

"For an old broad!"

He chuckled. "I hope we'll still be friends. We okay?"

"We'll always be jazz buddies."

He barked out a quick laugh, then frowned. "Now, tell me what's happening with Alyssa?"

As I filled him in on the saga, I must have looked ready to blubber, yet again, because he put his arm around me, patting my shoulder. Even his eyes looked watery.

"When is this intervention? Do you want me to come?"

The coffee pot was making fizzy noises and the aroma made my mouth water. I needed liquid to continue talking—and a little space. "Coffee first, please." After he poured two mugs and added cream, we went out to his porch and I told him my team was ready to go; we just needed Jake, the intervention guy, to get everything set up.

"You're a brave, strong woman. If I can help your daughter, in any way, you *will* let me know, right?" He choked up and cleared his throat. "It would make me feel...better...about...you know." He looked broken, his face collapsing. "Alyssa makes me think about my daughter, and...if I could help her, well, damn, I'd feel..."

I reached over and took his hand—no sofa hugs today. We sat quietly for a few minutes, a strong upright bass sound thumping with faster and faster riffs.

As I stared into my coffee an epiphany swamped me. I was the one who should go get Alyssa—right now, before she ODed or— Why hadn't I flown to New York the day Quinton found her? Observing Bob's permanent grief over his daughter's death injected me with a new power and a fevered need to reach Alyssa right that minute. I didn't want remorse to ruin the rest of my life.

I leaped out of my chair, startling Bob, sloshing my coffee over both of us. "I've just decided—this minute—I'm getting on a plane to New York and I'm bringing her back here. Right now!" I was breathing in short gasps—hopefully not another panic attack. "I know it's right. Alyssa would never come to an intervention."

"Then I'm coming with you—no choice. I can get some Suboxone, got a friend on it, in case she's in withdrawal when we get there."

"No! I can't put you in danger. I'm gonna call Quinton. He's a big, scary guy—and her husband."

"Yeah. Then why hasn't he already done this? Listen, I need to come with you—for me as much as for you and Alyssa."

"I don't know—let me make some phone calls. Can you really leave tomorrow morning, with ER and—"

"Consider it done. I'm owed a lot of favors. Come back here in a couple of hours and we'll make plane reservations. And thanks for letting me help, my jazz friend."

Back home, my first call was to Quinton, who answered after several rings. Without any preamble, I asked, "Will you go with me and a friend tomorrow to try to get Alyssa on a plane back to Florida?"

He sputtered a few unintelligible words, then said, "This Darius she's living with, he's a mean SOB—she lived with him before, you know; she might not want to leave." He paused. I thought he'd hung up. "Okay, shit, I'll come. Ah, what about your intervention? Isn't that safer?"

"Too complicated. Too many people. I know I'm the one who got on that path, but I was terrified. Now, I'm afraid to wait a day."

My last call was to Leo and I was relieved when his voice mail answered. I didn't want to argue with him—he would not want me to go, or he'd want to come. I didn't have time to explain everything—especially about Bob coming. Not only was Bob younger, but I knew he needed to be the rescuer. And Alyssa knew him. So I resorted to the white lie. My message said I was driving over to Naples tomorrow for an overnight visit with a sick friend. I'd tell Susan tonight since I was joining her for dinner—that would be argument enough.

Bob phoned me two hours later and we met at his computer to purchase our tickets to JFK. When I arrived he asked, "You still want to do this?"

"Positive. Every cell in my body is telling me to go."

"I really meant it, you know, about caring about you, just—"

"Bob. I think I'm in love with Leo. Don't worry. You've helped me in a lot of ways I can't even explain, so…we're good, okay!"

He asked me to put the Suboxone he'd procured in my purse. We hugged and planned to meet at 7 a.m. to catch the 9:45 flight. Bob reserved a minivan to pick up at the airport—I wasn't sure why he wanted such a large vehicle, but I didn't ask.

My "date" with Susan was for our usual Chinese takeout. By the time I knocked on her door, I was running on pure adrenaline. Susan yelled, "Hurry up. That Wok It Out joint already delivered. Grab a wine and sit your *tuchis* down." She had everything set up so we got right to work on the boxes—after all, we'd been having dinner together for over fifty years. Chinese takeout had been our dorm room treat.

I tried to get a word in, but Susan was quicker on the draw. "Before we eat, in keeping with my personal tradition: Two Chinese men are walking out of Katz's Delicatessen. One says to the other, 'The problem with Jewish food is that two weeks later you're hungry again.'"

I tried to laugh with Sue while trying to chew—only good friends eat that way, with lo mein noodles hanging out of their mouths. Sue was in such an upbeat mood, I didn't want to start in again with my problems. She burbled on about Michael, where they went, how much time they were spending together, while I labored at eating. When we were finished stuffing our faces, I asked, "So, you and Michael, doing *it* yet?"

"We are actually talking about doing the big *it*—as in matrimony. Don't laugh."

"Wow. Wow. That's wonderful...I'm happy for you. And I'm maid of honor, of course?"

"If we don't elope. He's a widower—he had a happy marriage to a woman who never worked, just took care of his home, his two boys, and fed them all too much." She paused, and stared at me. "Ahem. Again, you're not noticin'?"

"No. I mean, yes, I did notice how great you look. Just got into the food before I...and I'm preoccupied with, you know, my messy life."

"Sure, *bubala*, just teasin'. But Michael and I, we're gonna get healthy together. I can't believe what I'm saying, but I love him. How mushy is that at age seventy? Can you believe?"

"Well, my friend, *mazel tov*."

Finally Susan sensed my vibrating body and nervous eye movements because she asked, "Okay. Out with it. You ready to launch yourself to the moon or somethin'?"

I told her my plans for the next day with Bob and Quinton.

"*Oy vey!* That sounds way too dangerous. Let the pros do this."

"I have to go; I have to try!" I put my head down on the table.

"Maureen, *bubala*. No way. Are you just gonna barge in on a drug dealer? You crazy?"

"The guy went to Pratt and he's an artist too, not a real dealer, just dealing to get his fix. I'm going. I can't explain, but I feel like she's in too much danger to wait. And—"

"Then take me too. I can shout anyone down."

"You stay here. Bob and me and Quinton, we'll be the Three Musketeers."

"You know I love ya. I don't think you should go, but do what you have to. And keep me posted. Have you told Leo the Lionhearted? He'll probably have you committed."

"This sounds pathetic, but I lied to him to keep him here. I think he's too old to be involved in this. Told him I'm visiting a sick friend in Naples."

"Hmm. I'll try to calm old Leo while you're gone. Be careful!"

***

Back in my apartment, packing a few things in a carry-on, thoughts about Susan's upcoming marriage took my mind off my trip. I reminisced about my wedding for the second time that day. Susan had been my maid of honor although she *kvetched* before, during, and after. "I gotta wear a pink gown, with my figure—you nuts?" "You're goin' through with the full Catholic deal you don't believe in anymore?" "I am not dancing with the best man—I don't dance, period." My father would have gone apoplectic if I hadn't had the Roman Catholic mass with altar boys and music and communion. John said whatever made for easy family relations, he'd do. We had not yet joined a UU church back then, and my father's Irishness made his brand of Catholicism an emotional lethal weapon. We never told him about our un-conversion. He died thinking we were still in the fold.

Chapter 17

Saturday morning found me waiting outside Bob's apartment at seven, sipping tea from my travel mug, dressed in New York black, a purse and a backpack hanging from my left shoulder. It was cool for a Lauderdale April morning, so my layers of jackets would be perfect for the City. I'd checked the forecast and it would be raining and about fifty-five in Brooklyn. When I got up, I'd chugged a double-dose of Imodium to stave off my nemesis in stress and switched from coffee to tea for safety.

Calmness had settled over my brain once I'd made the decision to go to New York. Having Bob as a partner was an unexpected gift and boosted my hopeful feelings. He would be a friend for life after this, and Leo would understand why I had to lie and leave—I hoped.

Bob came out dressed in jeans, a black leather jacket, and black turtleneck. He looked strong and tough. I noticed the gray at his temples for the first time, accentuated by a gray cap. Details of the trip were already etching my brain. Why wasn't I terrified? A powerful strength of purpose infused me, driving out interfering thoughts.

We were taking my Prius to the airport; Bob did not want to leave his Porsche there. "Maureen, are you okay to drive?"

"Fine. Eerily fine—and without Valium. I'll drive; the Prius takes a little getting used to."

In the car, Bob found a jazz station and we were both silent. The traffic cooperated and was polite and light, probably because it was Saturday and the commuters were home in bed. We zipped through airport security, no long lines for a change, and waited for the flight. The airport, like all airports, pinged and bonged and announced constantly, which closed off thinking or talking. We both poked around on our phones, Bob giving me an occasional encouraging pat. On board, I had the window and Bob the middle seat, and we were finally up, up, and on our way.

I broke the silence, nudging Bob to get his attention. "If there is any sign of violence or danger when we get there, please don't go all Clint Eastwood on me, okay?"

"We have no idea what we'll find, but I'm not crazy. Your safety and Alyssa's, that's all that's important."

"And yours! I can never thank you enough for volunteering to do this with me."

"Like Haiti and the ER, I need to root out my demons. This will help me too, believe me."

In a trance, I followed Bob off the plane, over to Hertz, into our minivan, and off to 45th Street in Brooklyn to pick up Quinton. I'd phoned him from the car when we were close, so he was waiting outside. I jumped into the back since His Hugeness would fit better in the front. The two men shook hands and said brief hellos, eyeing each other like betters sizing up a horse. We stopped at a diner on Linden Boulevard for lunch—it was after one and the men were hungry.

We sat in a booth, Bob and I facing Quinton. A waiter dumped menus on the table. Bob turned, looked at me, and said, "You make sure you eat something, okay. Don't want you fainting on us."

For some reason we were all living in a cloud, which hid the frightening reason for our trip. Where was the panic I thought I'd be feeling? That I should have been feeling! We didn't have much of a plan—but Bob said he was working something out in his head. Were the guys just covering up anxiety? No, I thought—they were not actors. Maybe it was the male drive to rescue the damsel in distress.

Bob and Quinton ordered big burgers and fries. I asked for an egg and toast. Nice and bland. Digestive safety was important. Needing a bathroom at an inopportune time might be problematic under those unknowable circumstances.

Quinton spoke about our mission. "I tried to call Darius a few more times, but he musta blocked my calls after that first one. We know each other slightly. We're both part of the Brooklyn art scene, but I think Darius is just a druggie now. Ya know they lived together before, right?"

"I figured it was the same guy even before you told me."

Bob said, "I'm sorry, but I gotta ask. Are you sure this isn't jealousy or revenge on your part? Do you know for sure about Darius's drug use and Alyssa's?"

"I don't know how they're financing their use, but I know from friends of friends they've been seen high and they've been spotted purchasing and selling. And none of Alyssa's friends have been able to reach her—not by email or text. Both are strung out and needing a fix a lot of the time."

Bob asked, "Why haven't you gone to this address and tried to talk to Alyssa?"

"I did once. Saw them on the street near their apartment. She screamed at me to get lost. You probably think I'm a wuss. I had a run-in with Darius about a year ago; he had some buddies beat the shit out of me and that was over his art. I still think you're crazy to be goin' in there, Maureen! You too, Bob."

"I'm her mother. I don't believe this Darius guy will risk hurting me, so I'm going to sit by their door till I see my daughter. Why don't you stay in the—I hate to use the expression—the getaway car."

Bob stood up. "Okay. The getaway-car person will call the police if we don't come out of there in half an hour. Now, do what you need to do. Let's get going. Quinton, why don't you drive? You know the way, right?"

We piled back into the van, with Quinton driving and me up front next to my secret son-in-law. He took the Gowanus to the BQE, which both had light traffic for a weekend afternoon. I finally had the nerve to ask the most painful question. "Quinton, you said she was prostituting herself. Are you certain that's true?"

"No, no, not for sure. She was seen with Darius in some spots known for pickups, but, shit, who knows?"

I leaned against the car door and closed my eyes. Twenty minutes later we were parked in front of a stone building etched by years of pollution in an area with street after street of old warehouses.

It was drizzling. I looked up and down the gray, deserted block. Ancient ten- to twelve-story buildings lined both sides. Most buildings had loading docks; trash littered the sidewalks and a giant dumpster was in front of Alyssa's ugly building. The only sign of life was a sidewalk sale of old office equipment next door—two young Hispanic guys, ogling us, lounged on the desk chairs under umbrellas, their feet propped up on the battered metal desks they were selling—or were they selling something else? No sign of customers.

Bob said, "Let's all set timers in our phones for thirty minutes. Quinton, you stay in the van. Call my cell when the timer goes off. If I don't answer with 'Hiya,' call the cops and send them up." Bob's plan sounded pretty good—I was impressed. We all set our timers; Bob and I set ours on vibrate. I thought, *I could be killed in less than thirty minutes.*

Then we had to find Alyssa. There was a small door to the side of the loading dock with buzzers to each unit. Quinton said the building had been converted from a warehouse to art studios, and Darius was living there illegally. I buzzed 7F a few times. No voice sounded through the intercom, and no answering buzz sounded to get us in the door. I walked over to the local "sales force" and asked if they could help me get in to find my sick daughter. I think my sincere fear and misery inspired them to answer.

"Lady, just hit all them buttons. Some jerk'll buzz ya in."

I started on the top button and pressed ten of them quickly; within a minute someone buzzed us in without asking who was there. Bob held my hand as we walked down a worn-out corridor. At the end of the dark passage we saw the only way up was an old-fashioned freight elevator with a heavy metal door blocking the entrance. Bob pressed the call button and grinding sounds emanated from the open shaft. *Thank God for Bob.* Operating that old elevator, when it finally came down to us, was beyond my strength, and I would never have figured out how the outer and inner doors worked.

We shuddered up to the seventh floor in an elevator you could fit an elephant in, and it jolted to a stop—not quite on the level of the floor. As Bob pulled the heavy metal doors open, my artificial calm began to dissolve.

Bob noticed my hesitation and heavy breathing. "You okay? Still want to do this?"

I gulped more air. "Yeah. Deep breaths are helping. Let's go." I hoped another panic attack was not brewing. My stomach was sending out enough acid to bore through steel. My emotions always showed up first in my gut, so I was always armed with Imodium, Tums, and Prilosec.

The seventh floor had only two working lights and seemed purposefully labyrinthine with its unexpected dead ends. The building filled my nostrils with old dust—I was choking, my nose and throat already raw. The floors were cracked concrete painted over years ago, the paint flaking off. I'd probably die of lead poisoning.

We arrived at an industrial metal door with 7F barely visible. There was no doorbell, so I knocked, the metal biting my knuckles, the sound echoing up the corridor. No one answered. Bob took over and hammered on the door with his fist a couple of times.

We looked at each other and shrugged. "Maybe no one is there," I said. My courage was seeping out with each second that passed. My head snapped up when we heard a male voice behind the door.

"Yeah. Who the fuck's there?"

I cleared my throat and few times and croaked, "I'm Alyssa's mom. I just got here from Florida to see her."

"She don't wanna see you."

I took a deep breath. "I want to see her."

He opened up a crack, keeping the chain locked. I peered at a thin, light-skinned black man with a shaved head, wearing a wife-beater to show off arms covered in tattoos of entwined bodies. He was handsome but scary in the way he glared at me, then looked Bob up and down.

"Who the fuck's he?"

"He's a friend. Can I see Alyssa now?"

"How'd you find us anyway, Mommy from Florida?"

"Quinton told me where you are."

"Ol' Quinton the husband! Hah! What a loser. She don't need him."

I ramped up my voice, hoping to sound determined. "Look. Alyssa needs her mother. I want to see her now."

"Take your boyfriend and get the hell outta here. She'll call ya when she wants to." He spoke softly, but with venom in his voice.

Bob's deep voice echoed down the corridor. "Darius, we'll have the police following you everywhere if you don't open up. You want to see a cop behind you every time you go out? That'll happen if we don't see Alyssa now."

Darius's eyes narrowed and he hissed at us under his breath. "She don't want you in her life. Go back to Florida!"

He does not want Alyssa to hear him, or us. I wasn't going to let an angry addict scare me away. I screamed, loud enough to be heard across the East River, "Alyssa! Alyssa!"

An answering "Mom? Mom, is that you?" came from behind Darius.

Although he had to look up at Darius, Bob's melodious baritone sounded like a tough TV cop. "You don't want the kind of trouble I can bring down on you. Open up."

Darius closed the door in our faces but lifted the chain lock, then let us in. We walked past him into a huge high-ceiling room with a curtained-off section about thirty feet from the door. Tall windows with no covering except dirt let in dim light, illuminating stained concrete floors and a makeshift kitchen area on an upper level. The stench of vomit and stale cigarettes assaulted my burning nostrils.

Two sagging dirty-brown sofas and a huge TV, surrounded by trash and dirty dishes, filled one wall. Four large acrylic paintings of grotesque female nudes were propped against the wall. What trash—and Darius thought of himself as an artist.

"Alyssa!" I shouted. The curtain parted and I swallowed hard, trying to hide my shock and panic. She was wearing dirty jeans and a huge sweatshirt, but I could tell she'd lost every fat cell since I'd last seen her. Her body was a vibrating skeleton in clothes. Her hair—what was left of it—was standing up in clumps.

Her hoarse voice said, "Mom...what...how did you..."

"I came to take you home with me. Right now."

"I can't. Go...you don't want me. I'm a terrible person...this is where I belong." She could barely stand up; she looked like a zombie.

I heard myself moaning, "Ah, ah, ah..."

Bob spoke, since I was dumbstruck. "Alyssa. I'm Bob. I drove you to your Mom's one night, remember?"

Her weak little voice said, "Yeah. Nurse Bob."

At least some of her brain cells must still be working.

"We're here to take you home now. Any help you need, we'll find it." Bob's voice returned to his reassuring rabbi tone.

Darius, who had been surprisingly silent, said, "Al. You don't have to go with them. We're doin' fine."

I got my voice back. "Quinton is in the car waiting. Just get your things. We can buy anything you need. Okay, hon? Please."

Alyssa doubled over. "Mom...you don't know...Quinton—he doesn't know...I aborted our child when I left him. He didn't even

164

know I was pregnant—he'll hate me." She started coughing so hard, I thought a lung would pop out. She was obviously in withdrawal and sick. When the hacking stopped, she said, "It would've been damaged, y'know, by the shit I've been taking…"

Now she was sobbing. Staggering over to the sofa, she fell down in a twitching mass and curled into a ball, probably to hide her shakes. Darius shouted at us, "Get the fuck out! She's gonna stay with me!"

I went up to Darius and screamed into his face, "No!" I scurried to the sofa, took Alyssa's hand, and pulled her into the curtained-off area. She weighed nothing; I could have carried her. She couldn't resist. Behind the curtain was the not-unexpected mattress on the floor, messy blankets on top of sheets that never visited the laundry, clothes mounded all around. Alyssa fell into a beat-up barrel chair.

"Pack up what you need from here. I love you and I'll…" I couldn't get more words out, my tongue a roll of gauze in my mouth. The air was worse behind the curtain—cheap perfume mixed with sewer stench.

"I need a…a, y'know, a fix." She looked at her lap. "And I've got the flu or something. A fever. I've been puking for two days. Nothin' left in me."

"I have Suboxone. Bob said an eight milligram dose might be right." I fumbled in my purse and pulled out one pill. I was afraid to show her the bottle.

A dirty hand with chewed nails reached up and grabbed the pill. Instead of swallowing it, she put in on a piece of paper and smashed it with a mug, then poured the powder under her tongue. She said, garbled, half her tongue not moving, "Takes a while to dissolve, longer to work."

I heard a rumble of male voices near the door and hoped Bob was controlling the Darius scene. I perched on the arm of my daughter's chair, afraid to sit anywhere else. She shrank away but I picked up her hand and stroked it. "I love you and I will do everything I can to help you." She let me hold her hand while she suppressed her coughing. Even her hand was hot. Maybe we needed to go straight to a hospital.

A few minutes later Bob came to the curtain and asked to come in. I told him, "She's got a fever, a bad cough, just finished two days of bad stomach flu, no food, maybe dehydrated."

Bob stood in front of Alyssa. "Hey. Darius left. Can I feel your head, take your pulse, listen to your heart?"

She nodded yes.

Bob whipped out a stethoscope I had no idea he'd brought and examined her. Alyssa was shaking less and breathing better. Her eyes stayed down. Bob's warmest voice asked, "Alyssa. Will you come with us? I've got Suboxone and some other meds in the car. I have a good buddy who's a physician at a local clinic. I think we can get you checked out without going through ER. Okay?"

I was relieved Darius had left, but I hoped he didn't find Quinton. Bob and I perched on either chair arm next to Alyssa, waiting for her pill to dissolve. Finally she swallowed and asked me to go into the bathroom with her. I tried not to breathe in the tiny half-bath and watched while she rinsed out her mouth a few times and splashed water on her face. A transformation had taken place since she'd ingested the Suboxone. Her shaking was almost gone; she was still weak, but her eyes focused again. She peed—I needed to go also, but would have rather done it in the street than there.

"Got anything you want to grab before we go?"

In the "bedroom" she lurched around and stuffed some old clothes into her backpack (I hoped bedbugs and roaches were not included), shoved her feet into shoes, put on a parka, then took my hand again. She needed help walking; she'd become an old toddler. I remembered walking her chubby, healthy body out of daycare everyday—her bright smile and precocious verbalizations. At age three, she'd composed a poem for me: *Mommy, please dance with me, so we can always be, together and happy.*

We passed silently by the disgusting mess and made it into the elevator—which surprisingly was still on floor seven—Darius must have run down the stairs—and clanged downward. The outside air, even with the rain, smelled pure. We climbed into the van just as my cell vibrated, telling me the half hour was up—a half hour that had felt like a jail term.

Chapter 18

Quinton drove a few blocks and pulled over. In the back seat, I held Alyssa's hand and stroked her shoulder, her head leaning onto my shoulder. She reeked—toxic BO mixed with whatever stained her jeans and sweatshirt. No one had said a word yet.

Quinton turned around to look at Alyssa. "Baby, we all wanna help. Your mom, here, she's real brave—braver than me."

Alyssa squeaked out, "Sorry...so sorry, y'know, for..."

Bob had already called his doctor friend. "Steve, Dr. Wright, can see us now. He'll stay at his office till we get there." He looked back at us. "Alyssa, hey, I think you'll be all right, but you're dehydrated and still feverish. This doc is a cool dude. We worked in Haiti together. Okay?"

She glanced up at Bob and nodded yes, then let her head drop back down. He handed her a bottle of water and told her to take small sips, then used his phone to get directions to the Park Slope address. He navigated for Quinton. When we found the building in an upscale area, Quinton told us to go on in—he'd find a place to stay with the van. He seemed embarrassed to be near Alyssa. Bob and I each took one of Alyssa's arms and guided her into a lobby and down a corridor to Dr. Wright's office. He met us at the door of his empty clinic and greeted Bob with a bear hug. He was a huge, hairy man, dwarfing Bob. He was young for a doctor, too—not more that thirty-five, I guessed, with a dark beard and warm cow eyes. After introductions, which I think bewildered the good doctor, he asked Alyssa if I could stay with them in the exam room. Again, she nodded yes.

The doctor had Alyssa put on a gown and the sight of her arms and what I saw of her back and legs made me cry out, "Oh, my baby girl," and sit down before I fell. She had bruises of various colors all over her body.

Dr. Wright, who said to call him Steve, gently asked, "Alyssa, who did this to you?"

Whimpering, in a whisper, Alyssa told us, "Darius. He hit me cause I wouldn't let him sell my, ah, services. And I had to have Vikes or Oxies. That pissed him off. He wanted me to shoot heroin with him. You know, at first he said he'd help me get clean, but he sold my bupe, y'know, my Suboxone. He threw out my cell phone or I lost it. Not sure. I'm sure he took my wallet, my license. When I got sick—first just coughing, then fever, then the barfs, he treated me like shit. He dragged me with him, all the time, even when I was too sick to get up and was puking in the street. Sometimes he'd get me pills, sometimes..." Her voice got weaker and weaker and just ran out.

Dr. Steve looked close to tears himself. The Suboxone had fixed some of Alyssa's symptoms—she was no longer jumpy. Skinny and pale, but less ashen than when we first saw her, she hid her face in her hands.

"Doctor, Steve, can we take her straight to Florida, to my place? We can drive there in eighteen hours. She has no ID so we can't fly. Bob and, um, another guy will drive. What do you think?"

He directed his answer to Alyssa, which I liked, "Well, Alyssa, I'd like to take some blood right now and send it out to a place that will rush it through for me, but I think you can make the trip. Your heart and blood pressure are okay. Your temp's not too high. Can you keep liquids down, like Gatorade?"

"I think so. I drank water on the way here."

"Get to a doctor ASAP when you get home. Sip Gatorade all the way. Eat some popsicles. Try some ginger tea to soothe your stomach, then take Advil for pain and fever after you get a banana or some yogurt down." He gave us both a smile. "If it's okay with you, I'll talk to your nurse, Bob. Get dressed now and we'll meet you outside."

In the waiting room, Alyssa slumped onto a sofa, so Steve talked to Bob and me. "If you want to drive straight through, get lots of Gatorade. Start her on some popsicles too, or ice chips, some very bland food, like broth or bananas, some plain yogurt later on. And call 911 if her fever spikes while she's on the Advil. I'll email you the results of her blood tests, but I believe just forcing sports drinks down her will get her electrolytes back in order."

Bob said, "Thanks, Steve. I thought she could make it, but I'm no doctor."

"You're better than most docs! She's lucky to have you both."

I sighed with some relief and asked, "Steve. How can I thank you?"

"You just call me when you get to Florida. Let me know what's happening."

He gave Bob a friendly punch. "And Bob, I'm going back to Haiti, this'll be the fifth time. You want to come?"

When Bob said he'd love to go back, I felt a pang. No, not a lovesick pang, but we—I—needed him. Hopefully he would not run off too soon.

***

Back in the car, we all started to speak at once. Quinton came to life and took charge. "We can stop at my apartment and pick up pillows, food, water, ice, and Gatorade." He looked behind him at his wife. "And lots of your clothes are still there, Alyssa. Anything else anyone can think of?" We were all too drained to respond. Quinton added, "We should get right on the road. Saturday night and Sunday should have light traffic."

Alyssa touched Quinton's back. "I know it sounds lame, but I am sorry, for everything. You don't owe me...I owe you...but I can't talk about stuff yet. Okay?"

Quinton reached back and patted her hand. His voice was husky. "Just get well. We can talk when you're ready."

We parked near Quinton's apartment and followed him in to use the facilities and pack for our twenty-hour adventure. If anyone had told me I'd be nurturing my drug-addicted daughter on this mother-of-all-motherhood-nightmare journeys, I'd have said, *Not possible.* But there I was, peeing and fixing my face in Quinton's neat little bathroom, then helping pick out necessities for the trip. Stinky Alyssa took a shower, thankfully. Her smell had begun to pollute the car. In clean clothes that were way too big for her, with wet hair, she looked like a tiny, pale copy of my lovely daughter, but one hundred percent better than a few hours ago.

As we loaded in food, drink, bedding, and an ice chest, I finally understood why Bob had rented a minivan. Bob and Quinton had the macho debate over who would drive and who would sleep. Both of them were, of course, fine to drive. I told them I could drive too, once we were out of the New York area. The show was on the road, with Alyssa sipping Gatorade and eating saltines, me eating a PB&J sandwich, and the guys—both too wired to sleep—navigating out of the city. It was still light, still drizzling, and still gloomy. I would relax again after we got Alyssa to Florida and to a doctor.

***

After about three hours of driving, Quinton said he needed to stretch out in the back of the van for a while and try to sleep, and we all needed to stop and stretch and pee. Alyssa had fallen asleep with her head in my lap. I was a frozen pretzel of discomfort.

When we pulled off the interstate into a truck stop, we were almost to Baltimore. It was after nine, dark and still raining. I gently

woke Alyssa and we headed straight to the women's room, then met the guys, who had ordered burgers and fries for the second time that day—they'd need Lipitor by time we arrived in Florida. How could they eat that fatty stuff and sit in a car? Bob told Alyssa she should have a banana and some plain yogurt, or maybe some chicken soup if she felt up to it. She and I both ordered some soup—my stomach could only survive bland food.

Sitting at a round table, surrounded by mostly-male truckers eyeing our little gathering, we were all subdued and concentrated on eating. I got out my phone and walked over to a private area to listen to voice mail and check email. There were three voice messages from Leo—no surprise there—and one from Susan. I'd had my phone turned off for most of the trip, so I started with the oldest Leo message: "Maureen. What's going on? I saw you leaving with Bob this morning and I don't know what to think."

The second message said: "I just saw Susan. She said you went to Brooklyn with Bob. I don't know what to say, except...I'm deeply hurt."

He'd left the third message only a few minutes earlier: "For God's sake, call me. I talked to Susan again. Are you crazy? Going to confront a drug dealer. I'm beside myself. Call!"

I was not ready to have a conversation with Leo so I emailed him:

To: Leo Silverman
Subject: Alyssa

Please, please trust me. I had to go and Bob wanted to help. We have Alyssa with us and we're driving home. She's going to need a Suboxone-licensed doctor right away, preferably one who's also a shrink and a GP. Can you set up appointments for her? We'll be home by late afternoon tomorrow if all goes well. I'll need about forty hours of sleep, then a good bottle of red wine.

Hugs, Maureen.

I wasn't sure how to end my email to Leo. I was *not* ready to sign off with *Love, Maureen. Hugs* did sound a bit silly—minor worries of life. I'd promised Susan I'd call, but it was 9:30 on a Saturday night so she was probably with Michael. I touched her number by accident (as common as butt-dialing) so I let it ring—she could allow it to go to voice mail if she was all huggy with her fella.

She answered with, "So you finally called. I'm gonna have a heart attack. What's goin' on?"

"Hello to you too, Sue."

She laughed at my rhyming mode.

"We've got her, and we'll be home tomorrow evening. I emailed Leo. He sounded kinda pissed off in his voice mails!"

"He only called me about ten times with questions: 'Why'd she go with Bob? Are they going out? Why'd she lie? Is she crazy? Why didn't she tell me?'" Sue's voice rose an octave with each sentence. *Damn.* "Don't ever do this again. We were both worried sick! Leo, maybe, about you and Bob, not just you doin' something dangerous."

"Okay, Sue. I hope *never* to do anything like this again. I aged ten years in one day. I love you. See you soon."

"Love ya too, *bubala*. Be careful, and good night."

***

Somehow Bob drove until sunup, with Quinton sleeping in the rear and me dozing on and off with my head on a pillow against the passenger door in front. Alyssa, who'd had another Suboxone during our rest stop, slept spread out in the back seat. I tried to talk to Bob every half hour or so to be sure he wasn't drifting off. I kept offering to drive, but he kept telling me to rest. He was constantly searching the radio dial every fifty or so miles as one station after another faded out. No good jazz.

About three in the morning I noticed the rain had stopped and the roads were dry. "Bob. Let me drive. You need a break and it's just empty highway."

"I'm used to long hours at work—done quite few double shifts in the ER, so I'm fine."

"I just realized Alyssa hasn't smoked since we found her. Maybe she quit?"

"Don't get your hopes up. There were piles of butts around that studio. She's probably weak and too afraid to ask. Also, the Suboxone takes away some anxiety."

I dozed again and woke up needing to pee badly. The sun was just visible. Alyssa was stretching out and yawning. Quinton was fumbling around in the back. We pulled off at a sign for Dunkin' Donuts. Bob said they always opened early. By the dawn's light we headed for Dunkin's bathrooms, me leading the charge. The men, of course, finished with the bathroom faster and had already ordered egg sandwiches, donuts, and coffee.

Alyssa said, "I know. No coffee. I'll just have the egg white sandwich and water and maybe a taste of a donut. Someone order for me. I'm gonna take another pill, so can't talk for awhile."

That was the longest speech she'd made in front of Bob and Quinton. Bob answered, "Good girl."

Quinton told her, "I'll order just before we go. You can eat in the van, okay?"

Alyssa nodded.

Bob was finally wiped out. "Hey, Quinton. I'll need your bed in the rear."

We were off again, with me next to Quinton, my buddy Bob in the sleeping compartment, and Alyssa eating in the back seat after she'd rinsed out her mouth a couple of times, spitting out the window. "Sorry. Suboxone tastes awful. Gotta get rid of that before I eat."

Chapter 19

After two more pit stops, we pulled into the Gardens about six. Hopefully everyone would be eating dinner and not watching our pathetic procession. Outside the van, we sorted through the accumulated mess and divided the contents. Quinton towered over us but seemed awkward and deferent. He kept looking from his feet to the sky. Bob, our unacknowledged leader, said, "Quint, stay with me tonight—I know you need to get back. I'll get you to the airport tomorrow."

Bob looked over at me. "I'll pick up your Prius, unless you—"

I handed my key to Bob. "You don't use the key gadget; as long as it's in your pocket, the door will unlock when you get close. Just press the Power button to start it. Keep your foot on the brake when you start it and when you put it in gear. Gear shifting is just a flip up for Reverse and a flip down for Drive on the tiny shifter. Press Power again to turn it off. Thanks."

Alyssa was leaning against the van, still avoiding any close encounters with Quinton. Suddenly she went over to him, looking up into his face, and said, "Quint, thanks. I'll pay you back, y'know, for everything. I promise."

I was afraid the giant would cry. He said, "Don't worry, babe, just get clean and get well."

I felt guilty letting Bob do even more for us and offered to take the van to the airport so he did not need another day off. "Another day off is not a problem. You and Alyssa get some sleep. And what about doctors?"

"I already got an email from Leo. He's set up two appointments for tomorrow—one is with his son."

Bob winked at me and grinned. He knew about Leo and me—I hoped there still was a Leo and me.

Even though we'd just traveled over a thousand miles together, when the four of us squeezed into the small elevator it felt uncomfortably close, and we all smelled too ripe. Al stood in the corner using bags as a barricade and we escaped to our apartments like mice to their safe holes.

My condo was the Taj Mahal after our safari from New York. We dropped our bags on the floor and headed for the kitchen. I didn't ask, just pulled out two yogurts and a couple of bananas. We ate standing up and silent. I told Al, "Wake me if you need anything. I'm taking a long, hot shower, then passing out. And I'm turning off all phones after I call Aunt Sue and, ah, another friend."

***

When is a shower nirvana? When you're exhausted and so filthy you can see the dirt washing off. Later, when I no longer smelled like a homeless bag lady, I called Susan. No answer, so I left a message. "Don't call me until I've slept for twelve hours. We're home and okay, for now. And we could use your help tomorrow for transportation to Alyssa's doctors."

There were two voice mails from Leo, both said to call as soon as we arrived. I could not put it off any longer. I sat propped up in bed with a tall glass of OJ on my nightstand and dialed Leo's number. He, no surprise, picked up on the first ring.

"Maureen. God, I was so worried and…so damn angry. Can you come down for a drink to talk?"

"I'm way too exhausted. I haven't slept in two days. And I'm afraid to leave her."

"Can I drive you and Alyssa to the doctors tomorrow?"

"Thank you, thank you, for setting that up, but we'll go with Susan. It's just too soon for me to introduce you to Alyssa, I think. Does your son know her story?"

"Yeah. The basics." He cleared his throat in his change-subject manner. "I have to ask. Is there anything between you and Bob-the-Rescuer? I mean, he must care about you to take off like that."

"You have to talk to Bob. His need to help has to do with a very personal trauma in his past. And we're just friends who like jazz."

"I want to believe that! When can I see you? A drink tomorrow after dinner?"

I agreed to see Leo the next evening as long as Alyssa seemed strong and didn't need me. I was doling out our last few Suboxone pills to Alyssa, but we'd be seeing a doctor tomorrow for more.

I took one Valium, then hid the rest in the bottom of a tissue box. I fell into a deep sleep. I woke when sunlight brightened my room—it was after eight. I had slept for twelve hours. A record snooze. We had Dr. Ben's appointment at noon and Dr. Martha Whiting at three. I got up and put myself together for a momentous day—the beginning of Mommy's Rehab.

I made a big pot of coffee and ate a huge breakfast of scrambled eggs and toast. With my second cup of Joe, I caught up on emails and enjoyed sitting quietly on my porch—the morning sun pouring in was a delight after our gray, drizzly trip. At ten, I was ready to call Alyssa when she came out to the porch dressed in baggy, but clean, capris and a pretty blouse. Her hair needed a professional makeover and some new growth, but at least it was shiny clean. She'd put on a little makeup so her pale face looked healthier.

"Mom. I'm sorry. I never wanted you to know about any of this shit. I was ready to change when I came here—got back on the wrong track in Brooklyn."

"Sit down. Can I get you some real food? Are you okay?"

"Feeling better. Had another yogurt and some toast about seven, and some juice. I'm okay. What about doctors? I heard you and Bob talking."

"A good friend set up two appointments for today. First one is with an internist—my friend's son. Second is with a psychiatrist who can prescribe Suboxone—he had to really pull strings to get that one."

"Who's this *good* friend with the connections?"

"I've been dating him. Leo Silverman. Nothing serious."

"Hmm. Silverman and Goldman, really, Mom?" She raised her eyebrows at me. "I thought you and Bob had something goin' for sure. Why'd he come with you and do all this if he's not your boyfriend?"

"You'll have to talk to him someday. He's a rescuer. Worked saving lives in Haiti; works in the ER. It's something personal for him to explain."

"I hate to ask, and I know you'll never trust me with money again. But I need some cigarettes, and some Nicorette too. I'm cutting down, but now's not the best time to try to cold-turkey the cigs."

"Can you wait till we head to our first appointment? We'll stop on the way."

***

Susan arrived at our door at eleven, but her usual ebullient self dissolved when she saw Alyssa. She gave me an eye roll, then walked over to Alyssa and gave her a long hug. "Sweetheart, my favorite girl in the world, you gotta get better. And you better eat before you disappear. You listenin' to me?"

"I know. I've been trying. I know it doesn't seem like it. This time, y'know, it'll work out."

"I...let's get goin', you two." Susan at a loss for words: a rare occurrence.

We made a nicotine stop at a drug store and watched from the car as pale, skinny Alyssa smoked a cigarette down to the filter in

Guinness-record time. She returned to the back seat and Susan hit the accelerator. Alyssa suppressed a cough and said, "Sorry about the stink. I'm gonna try with the gum, maybe the patch, to cut down."

I said, "Al, right now that's not your or our biggest worry. Let's see what Dr. Silverman says."

I thought Susan would drive off the road. "Dr. Who? Are we...huh?"

"It's Leo's son, Ben. He's a physician. And a *mensch*. I've met him."

Now Alyssa poked me from the back. "I don't know if I'm comfortable with a doctor who's your *boyfriend's* son. Will he report everything I say?"

"I am sure Ben will keep doctor-patient confidentiality. You ask him. Really, they both did us a big favor." I let the boyfriend comment go by—the quote "doth protest too much" stopped me.

"Okay, okay. It just sounds sort of cozy. Do you know this shrink too?"

"No. Even Leo doesn't. It took him all day to find a doctor who could prescribe your medicine and who had an opening. If you don't like either one, we'll look for other docs. Bob has contacts too."

I was angry and frustrated. I couldn't tell her that Ben might be in a special position to help, since he'd had the same problem. Would he tell her? Al looked better today; her complexion was brighter, her cough almost gone, and the shakes had disappeared. I'd given her another pill before Susan was due to arrive, and she'd disappeared into her bathroom for fifteen minutes while it dissolved, I assumed.

a curried chicken sandwich, able to swallow only baby bites. Susan had a new phone and kept rechecking directions to Dr. Whiting's office. Maybe two appointments in one day was not such a great idea. The three of us loved each other but were uncomfortable under such strained circumstances. No one wanted to say the wrong thing.

Later Susan dropped us at Dr. Whiting's office and said to call her when we were finished—she'd be shopping at a T.J. Maxx she spotted. A young woman greeted us, said her name was Kristen, and gave Alyssa a questionnaire to fill out. Al cursed under her breath a few times while angrily scribbling notes on the forms. I kept my eyes on an old issue of *Time* magazine. Kristen came back in a few minutes and led Alyssa into the inner sanctum.

Two interminable hours later, Alyssa stood in front of my snoozing body, gave me a shoulder shake, and shouted, "Let's get out of here—now."

I jumped up and almost fell over. "Huh? What..."

"I hate this doctor. She's a witch. Got to find someone else."

As soon as we were out the door, I asked, "What's wrong? Did you get a prescription for Suboxone?"

"Yeah. And she wants a weekly pee test. And she wants me on lithium! I tried that shit—gave me the shakes. And I couldn't concentrate. Can we just go to a drug store, then home?"

Susan picked us up and we finally made it back to the Gardens. It was after five. I was reeling with exhaustion and worry. Sue insisted we all come to her place for some Chinese food. Al said she'd eat our leftovers. She had to go up and lie down.

The Chinese food came in less than ten minutes. Susan and I sipped Pinot Grigio while we waited. I told her about the blowup after the shrink appointment, the physical therapy, and the fact that I would soon be a taxi service for Alyssa.

"I hate to say this, *bubala*, but maybe Al should be in a rehab facility, not your condo."

"I have to give this a try. Day by day, okay?" I had never in my twenty-seven years of motherhood felt so momma-bear protective of my cub as I did now. Up until last month I'd assumed parenting was about over—my bird had fledged. Boy, was I wrong. Had I overlooked signs Alyssa would have such life-threatening problems? Were there any bipolar symptoms I'd missed?

The food was on the table and Sue said, "I'm out of Chinese-Jewish food jokes, but we need a funny. Lemme think." She paused, scratched her head, then said, "What did the Chinese waiter say to the table of Jewish women? 'Was anything all right?'" She laughed then shook her finger at me. "So, at least smile. I'm tryin' here."

When I got home it was six and Alyssa was asleep in her room. I could hear soft snoring noises. Damn, I'd forgotten to bring the leftover food home. I felt like an ancient cat that just wanted to curl up with its paws over its eyes. I looked into the mirror and knew I should not visit Leo—I needed a spa day, or spa week—but his most recent voice mail had said, "Got some icy limoncello and I bought a jazz album for you, recommended by a friend. See you later."

Chapter 20

After a shower and a new face application, I still saw the ancient mariner in my mirror, but I had to visit Leo after all he'd done for us. What I'd thought was just a little white lie to save him from danger had grown into a big *tzimmes*. Had I lied again when I told him there was nothing between Bob and me but friendship? Certainly that was now true. For reasons I could not lock down, the trip to Brooklyn had dampened my romantic feelings for Leo—or just dampened romantic feelings forever. Maybe it was because all my emotional reservoirs had been emptied by my total preoccupation with Alyssa. So why, oh why was I still so worried about how I looked? Was I doomed to suffer from each new line, wrinkle, and varicose vein till cremation? I would be cheerful company tonight!

At 7:30 I rang Leo's doorbell. *Breathe out and smile, Maureen.* He opened the door wearing the same blue shirt and white shorts I'd complimented him on a few days ago. (It felt like a few months ago. Time was playing tricks on me again.)

He examined me in doctor-mode, a frown, not a smile, on his face. "I wanted to stay mad at you, but you look like, like—"

"Don't say it. I know."

"Come. Sit." We sat on opposite ends of the soft leather sofa and he had a Ray Charles CD playing. "You lost weight in the last few days?"

"Yes. I'm so tired and emotionally drained—and involved in something I know so little about."

Leo walked to the open kitchen area and poured two drinks. He returned with the booze and sat back down a little closer. "You know I'll help you, don't you? That I've been through this. And..." He took a sip and harrumphed. "But first I need to know. Why did you lie? Sneaking off with Bob, I still feel—well, I don't know what I feel...should feel."

"I understand. I'm sorry. I know that might not get me off the hook, but it's true. I was afraid you'd want to come and I didn't want you to get hurt."

"Or get in the way because I'm an old fart?"

"Can we please get past this? It was a spur of the moment trip, maybe stupid, certainly not planned. And Bob, I can't tell you why, needed, wanted to be the rescuer—it concerns his past, not me or Alyssa. That's all I can say." I took a slug of limoncello and choked, almost spitting it across the coffee table. Not the way to drink a liqueur.

Leo patted me on the back and gave me tissues. "Maybe I assumed too much. Or maybe I'm too...damn it, Maureen. Come here."

I moved closer and he gave me an awkward but crushing hug, then took my hands in his. "Consider me past this. Just don't shut me out again, okay? And let me help in any way I can. Even something as simple as driving Alyssa somewhere. I have time, too much of it maybe."

I put my head on his shoulder and answered. "I promise. Let's listen to music for a few minutes. I need to get back to Mommy's Rehab soon."

Leo rubbed my arm, always an erogenous zone for me, but he confined the rubbing that time. We snuggled, and it was cloud nine for fifteen whole minutes.

Cloud nine dumped us when my phone blasted off, and I jumped up as though a brick had come through the window. It was Alyssa. "Mom. Where are you? I don't know how to use your damn alarm system and I'm starving."

"I'll be home soon. Just visiting Leo to thank him for his help. I forgot to bring the Chinese food, but you can scramble an egg. Oh, and my code is 1025, your birthday."

Leo walked me to the door, his arm around my waist. "I'm taking you to yoga tomorrow. And for a fattening breakfast after. See you at eight, right here, doctor's orders."

"I'm afraid to leave her. I keep thinking someone should be watching her day and night. Am I paranoid?"

"If she can't stay on the Suboxone program, then you'll have to get her into a rehab. I went through that with Ben. But she'd gotten herself on Suboxone when she came to you last month, and she came back with you. We'll see. You can go out to yoga—she probably won't get up till ten. Am I right?"

"You're right. She never comes out of her cave before eleven. See you in the morning. Good night."

He did not try to kiss me good night and I was relieved. I was numb to pleasure.

***

For the next few days I went to a yoga class every morning with Leo, and he practically force-fed me a healthy breakfast at the Goddess Café each day. No longer merely scones and coffee, he ordered oatmeal or yogurt or eggs, and he followed the same regimen with me. He then lectured me on vitamins, supplements, and what I needed to eat for lunch and dinner. I gained the lost weight back in three days and had to tell him to stop stuffing me—I'd need a new wardrobe soon.

We were right about Alyssa—she never got up before ten or eleven. I'd given her my old PC from storage and bought her a prepaid cell phone after she'd whined incessantly about keeping in touch with friends. She emailed all the people with whom she'd couch-surfed but no one could locate her passport or driver's license. I had to nag her for days to cancel her old passport, which she eventually did. She renewed, for a fee, her New York license, and it had to be sent to Quinton's since that was the address on it.

She never mentioned Quinton during our stilted conversations. I had to believe she no longer had feelings for him, nor, perhaps, he for her. After all, she had robbed him, gone back on drugs, and lived with that awful man, Darius. But he had come to Florida searching for her, and he was the one who located her when she disappeared, so he clearly still cared for her. Maybe they were emailing each other.

The cheap phone and old PC were beneath contempt for my high-tech daughter. "You know, I can't do any work without a MacBook Pro and the right software."

"Don't you have any idea where your old computer is?"

"Don't ask. It's gone! And Darius, he took my iPhone—I hadn't paid the bill in ages anyway."

"Oh, Alyssa. Get yourself healthy and then worry about work. You look—well, when we see Dr. Whiting again next week, how about going to my hairdresser?"

"I look like shit. I know." She ran her fingers through her damaged hair, bald spots showing in places. "Don't want some dowager hairdo though, y'know."

God, I hated her "y'know" tic. I hadn't heard her talk that way since middle school.

"And Mom? I called Nurse Bob. He's gonna look for another Suboxone doc for me. I can't stand Whiting; don't want to see her again."

"You've got to keep her until Bob finds another. Or you can go online and call Suboxone-licensed docs in the area. Bob and Leo told me they usually have waiting lists to get in to see them."

"Maybe Bob could get me my Suboxone—"

I tried controlling my anger. "No! You want to get him in trouble? Are you crazy?"

"Yeah. According to the last two shrinks."

***

On Monday, after another argument, Al agreed to see Dr. Whiting until she found someone else. Again I sat in the waiting room—sat, wrong word. I wriggled, paced, ate Tums (my sixth food group), picked up and put down five magazines. I was starting to resemble Alyssa in withdrawal. I practiced a few breathing meditations. I'd attempted to talk to her about her abortion, but she said she wasn't ready to discuss it. Later I'd brought up Quinton, and again, not ready. I certainly hoped the shrink was getting Alyssa to discuss something meaningful—I could not.

An hour later, Alyssa again stormed out, her voice out of control. "I hate that bitch. She's…" A paroxysm of sobbing cut her off. By the time we got outside, she asked me, "Mom. Do you think I'm bipolar? I'm sure not manic, y'know, maybe depressed, but who wouldn't be with their life so fucked up?"

"I don't know. Take your time. Probably Dr. Whiting is trying to get you to talk about your life and that makes you…uncomfortable." When I got no response, I said, "Let's get to the hairdresser—that's always good medicine. Okay?"

Damn, mommy training did not include Mommy-the-Shrink or Mommy-the-Rehab courses. Leo gave me a little advice at every breakfast, but I did not want to dwell on addiction every time we were together. We had not been out for dinner or any evening activity unless you counted the first night back. I'd promised him I'd eat at his place at least once that week and we wouldn't mention Al or drugs.

When I picked her up at the salon a couple of hours later, she looked better than I'd seen her in ages—she was a dark blonde with highlights and had added some lipstick. Together with the few pounds she'd put on, it was a miraculous reincarnation. I smiled. "You look so much better." She grunted back, fighting a grin that was trying to emerge. On the way home she asked, "So when am I gonna meet the famous Leo?"

I had been postponing the meeting—I didn't know why. Leo had seen her around the pool during her first stay. Was I afraid they'd hate each other? Would that make any difference to me—or to them? Alyssa deeply loved her dad, and Leo was John's opposite: John, big, strong, and uneducated, versus Leo, who was thin, intellectual, and old. Well, not old-old, young-old—healthy and active.

"We can ask him over for coffee and dessert after dinner some night." I was not ready for a formal sit-down dinner with us as a threesome.

"Now that I'm all fixed up, ask him for tonight."

She seemed all fired up to meet Leo. Strange.

Chapter 21

When Leo rang my bell at seven, I realized he'd never been in my condo before. I'd made decaf coffee and thawed out frozen brownies. Not fancy, but it was all I had. I was still surprised Al wanted to meet Leo at all, much less that night. Maybe the magic medicine of the hair salon worked. Leo had dressed formally for the occasion: good khakis, a blue button-down shirt, and real shoes. I had an awkward moment at the door—to hug or not to hug. Hmm, not. "Hi. Come in."

He handed me a box of chocolate mints and stepped into the foyer, peering into the great room. "Wow. I love your place. It's vibrant, like you."

He came into the living room and Alyssa said, "Dr. Leo, I presume."

She remained plopped in a big chair, so he walked over and held out his hand. It took her a few beats to shake it. "Hi, Alyssa. I've seen you a few times at the pool. Hope you get down there again soon."

"I'm a little freaked out about seeing your son as my doctor. I guess you know about most of my mess from Mom, anyway, right?"

"I do. And if there is any way I can help…well, I'll try."

I passed out coffee, then took orders for dessert. I had my supply of B&J's ice cream, but they each wanted only a small brownie. An uncomfortable silence held us all after I brought out the desserts. The clinking of forks sounded loud and violent.

When she'd finished her brownie, Alyssa asked, "So, Leo, you and my mom—"

The doorbell interrupted and I was surprised to find Bob standing there. I must have looked mystified or horrified, because Bob said, "Hey. Alyssa asked me to come over to talk. You didn't know? I can go."

"Gee. No. Come in. Want some coffee? It's decaf." *Shit, why did Alyssa invite Bob?* My stomach churned up some acid, choking me. Was she having a manic episode on top of her depression? Was that even possible?

Leo got up and shook Bob's hand and they exchanged some medical-hospital talk. When everyone found a place to sit, I said, hoping my incredulity didn't show, "Al. You invited Bob over. If you want some privacy to talk, you can use the porch."

Alyssa looked from Bob to Leo to me. "I just, I don't know, wanted to try to figure you all out. Your two Jewish men. Like, you come to New York with Bob, but you're dating Leo, but I know you dated Bob."

Leo scowled, then stood up, looked at Alyssa, and said, "I wish you the best, Alyssa. See you at the pool."

To me he added, "We'll talk later. Good night." And he walked out before I could even get up. Was my daughter really crazy? What could possibly have driven her to invite Bob and Leo over? She was hiding her face behind her hand. Was she smiling or frowning?

I stood up and glared at her. "Al. To use one of your terms, WTF?"

Bob hopped up. "I think you two need to talk—alone. Call me if you need me." And he exited. *Stage right* went through my brain. My life was a soap opera, after all.

I cleared my throat and took a sip of coffee so I wouldn't scream. "Why did you invite Bob and Leo over together?"

Her hand dropped down and I saw she was crying. "Bob's too young and Leo's too old and he looks so, so Jewish. Goldman and Silverman. God, Mom. A nurse and a doctor! How fucking weird. They're nothing like Daddy!"

I finally understood. She had always been a daddy's girl—her feelings of loss were finally emerging and trying to bury me. In the calmest voice I could muster I said, "First of all, I am not dating Bob. We went out once. Second, since when are you an anti-Semite? I'm appalled you said that. Third, Leo is only six years older than me and only two years older—" I didn't finish that one: only two years older than John would have been.

"I can't look at Leo and picture you two...together—I just can't. It makes me...angry. I don't know why. You know, there are so many obnoxious Jews in Brooklyn—those Hasids, Orthodox guys wandering around on Saturdays."

"God, Alyssa. Your Aunt Sue. You love her. She loves you."

"I love her too." She curled up on the sofa and faced the wall. "Just to think of Leo, like *with* you, y'know, like he was Dad." She cried some more. "I miss Daddy, every day. And I didn't help take care of him, when…I hate myself." She hiccupped a sob.

"I think we need to sleep on this and talk more tomorrow. Have you discussed any of this with Dr. Whiting?"

"Don't mention her." She grabbed her cigarettes and key and ran out.

I tried to call Leo after Alyssa left, but got his voice mail—a rare occurrence. I left a short message. "Leo. Sorry about Alyssa's weirdness tonight. And I only went out with Bob once, to a concert. Call, please."

After Alyssa slunk back in smelling of smoke, I took my computer to bed with me and watched reruns of *Doc Martin*—Doc always cleared my head of unhappiness—until I fell into a fitful sleep, my overheated computer tucked in next to my body.

***

I left a short message with Leo telling him I decided to skip morning yoga so I could lay in wait for Alyssa to emerge from her cave. I knew Leo was annoyed and upset because he always returned my calls immediately.

Could a delayed reaction to her grief have caused Alyssa to behave so badly last night? No one in my family had ever harbored anti-Semitic feelings, at least as far as I knew. Living in Brooklyn was not an excuse—even the Jews I knew were not fond of the Hasids. Susan called them the Jewish Taliban. Years of ingesting opiates might have affected her brain development—I'd read an article stating that.

As I sat on my porch sipping my second cup of coffee, hypnotized by the waving palm trees, Alyssa appeared and headed down for her morning dose of nicotine, which meant she'd already ingested her Suboxone. The doctor she hated had prescribed a new type that dissolved faster and with less terrible aftertaste.

I took a deep breath and touched her arm. "Hey. Can we talk, after your cigarette?"

She sat down next to me. "Okay. Talk about what? Daughter from hell? Fetus killer? Drug addict? Mentally ill?"

"Alyssa. Stop! What do you want? Don't you want to get well?"

"I just hate myself so much I think nothing matters. Nothing that happens to me matters."

"It matters to me, to Aunt Susan, to Aunt Tara, to Quinton, to your real friends."

"Yeah? None of them know about the abortion. Or how shitty I acted when Dad was sick. Most don't know about Darius. Poor Quinton. I can't believe he wanted to help me after the things I did to him."

"Obviously people love you and care. You need a good talk therapist for some of the rest. Do you want to stay here with me? Or would you rather be in a rehab?"

"Here." Her voice returned to little-girl mode. "And I don't know why I did what I did last night. Sometimes I want Dad so much and then I remember what a terrible daughter I was...when he needed me most. So I just hate everyone..."

"If you want to stay here, you'll need Dr. Whiting until you find someone else. Okay?"

"Somehow, y'know, she hit on my rawest spots right away. She asked about Dad and his death that first day. And...gotta have a cig, sorry." She bolted out the door.

***

My cell rang while I was cleaning and making a mental shopping list. I glanced at the caller ID and saw it was Leo. The temptation to ignore it was high, but I answered him. "Hi, Leo. I'm sorry—"

"Don't be. I should know better than anyone how impossible a recovering addict can be. It's okay. But think I'll keep a little distance from your daughter for a while."

"She's an emotional mess. Hates herself. God, will she ever be..." I couldn't add more.

"It's going to take time. Try to relax. About that dinner we were planning. Can you come over tonight? I want to be with you. I've missed you."

Chapter 22

At noon, Alyssa and I went out for lunch to a spot on an inland waterway and then to T.J. Maxx. She had lost so much weight none of her clothes fit. We agreed to not discuss *stuff* until she felt stronger. I told her I was going out for dinner and she nodded. I didn't mention with whom, and she didn't ask—perhaps she assumed correctly.

I spent a restful hour alone at the pool thinking about Bob and Leo. Bob had shown me I was still a sexy dame, although he obviously thought of me as a card-carrying, over-the-hill gal. Leo and I laughed often, even with all the *mishegas* in my life. Our humor bones were compatible—probably more important than our sex organs. And Leo was easy to be with—he made me want to cuddle. Was sex after seventy cuddling? I watched the cute little Florida lizards doing their mating dances, the males puffing the orange balloon under their chins in and out and chasing the females all over—or were the females chasing the males? Yesterday I was a voyeur as I observed two sandhill cranes mate by our lake—talk about a quickie—and soon alligators would be grunting for mates all over our peninsula. Everyone was doing it—wasn't that a song title?

At seven, looking chic in a black pencil skirt and a flowing silk shirt, I rang Leo's doorbell. Yes, I still cared about how I looked no matter how hard I fought against the need. He yelled, "Come in," and I found him in his kitchen sautéing veggies. He was more domestic than I.

"Hi. Can I help?"

"Pour us both a glass of the Merlot over there. And you can finish this while I put the lamb chops on the grill. Just stir." He gave me a peck on the cheek as he went out with a plate of garlic-covered lamb.

I poured, then stood stirring what appeared to be a ratatouille, which smelled of garlic and onion and some mystery spices. I flopped the veggies around in the black iron pan for a few minutes on high, tasted the yummy concoction, then turned down the heat. When Leo returned with the aromatic meat, we both filled plates in the kitchen and carried them out to a tiny table on the lanai.

"I meant to have a little cocktail time. I always start cooking too early. But it's pretty good, if I say so myself."

"It's delicious. You're a better cook than me. I believe in takeout Chinese and eating out...or eating here!"

"I'll bet you're a great cook. Maybe, like me, you don't like cooking for just yourself."

We sat quietly sipping our wine and watching an egret and a heron compete for fishing rights on the lake. The weather was warm, but a breeze kept it pleasant and wafted in the scent of the jasmine. I looked over at Leo. His was not a handsome face, but distinguished, with lively eyes and silver hair. His body was fit. I'd observed him at the pool for the past year, and at yoga for the past several weeks. For seventy-five, he was strong, flexible, and wiry—a runner's body with a bit too much tummy (like most of us).

We cleared the dishes together as though we'd been doing it for ages—a natural rhythm between us. He took my arm. "I'll finish this later. How about a limoncello and another *Doc Martin*? I'm up to season two. Okay?"

We sat on that soft sofa again, with the English seaside on the TV screen and Leo's arm around my shoulder. Leo laughed each time I covered my eyes to block out a bloody doctoring scene. "You'd never make a doctor or a nurse, sweetheart. How are you in an emergency?"

"Don't make fun. When Alyssa was five, I drove her to the doctor while holding a towel on her head—her blood dripping all over and her screams stopping traffic. Of course, I fainted once the doctor started stitching up her cut."

I kicked off my shoes, tucked my legs up, and leaned into Leo. I could imagine spending the rest of my life with him...if my life wasn't such a mess. I snuggled, and he began what he knew would start my engines—that circular stroking of my bare arm. I emitted a humming sound, not under my control.

His hand migrated from my arm up to my neck, then his fingers danced in and out of my right ear. In a short time I felt each touch on my ear as though his hand was between my legs. How did that happen? What connections! I didn't push him away.

As the credits from the *Doc Martin* episode rolled, Leo moved across my body and kissed me—this time no chaste kiss, but with a probing tongue and both hands holding my head. Oh, my, I was dizzy with desire only hours after thinking I did not want this—I did want this! What had happened to my intention of just cuddling? My love for Leo had been jumping forward three steps each time we were together, and, due to Alyssa, falling back two steps whenever we were apart.

In a husky voice, Leo said, "Can we take this into the bedroom?" He pulled me up and gave me a full-body kiss—he was obviously ready. As we walked toward his bedroom, my emotions made me dizzy and I wobbled and fell toward him. He picked me up and carried me to his bed—still strong enough to gently place me down. It was almost dark in his bedroom, thankfully, with a dusky light from the remains of sunset coming in through the shutters. Sitting next to me on the bed he said, "I want us to go slow and savor this. I've been watching you for over a year. Somehow I knew—honest—I knew we'd be good for each other."

I fully surrendered to my arousal, letting Leo undress me down to my bra and panties. I savored the touch of his hands through the silk of my bra, then he flicked his fingertips against my nipples, faster and faster, harder and harder, until I had a powerful orgasm from that alone. He kept asking me, "Sweetheart, what do you want me to do?" And I answered each time with, "What you're doing." I was never capable of sex talk—some Irish Catholic remnants remain forever.

His hands moved to my thighs, alternately tickling and caressing, getting closer and closer to home base. When he finally rubbed his fingers over my soft, damp panties, I screamed as wave after wave of orgasmic release pulsed though me. His hands were skilled, from doctoring or…

In the next instant, my agile yogi had slipped off my panties and entered me. In the waning light, he was a young Adonis, his hands holding mine over my head. I wrapped my legs tightly around him and heard him say, "I love you." We were teenagers again for a brief time.

My insides began to burn as the minutes wore on—and on. *If only he would finish*, ran though my mind. I made the mistake of opening my eyes and was shocked to see his mouth fixed in a grimace—like a heavyweight fighter in round twelve. Was a heart attack a possibility?

Damn, he must have taken Viagra or some new make-me-a-stallion drug. I was about to tell him I was in pain and he had to stop, when he moaned and fell on top of me. "Maureen, oh, Maureen."

We lay side-by-side, our bodies facing each other, both of us breathing heavily. When would I bring up his excess of prowess and my resulting damage? Maybe men think all women like them to bang away. Even women's magazines blab on about how great it is if your guy lasts at least ten minutes. Who did they interview?

But I would not discuss that—not during the mutual afterglow! I was too mesmerized by his hands stroking up and down my whole body. "You have the body of a woman half your age. And I'm not just saying that to have my way with you."

"Only in the dark!"

"No. Not only in the dark." He touched my lips with his fingertips. "I want to spend the rest of my life with you. You...you jazz up my life. I'm forty again."

"I want—"

I jumped up when I heard my phone ringing in the living room.

"Damn. I'll get your phone." His naked body scurried to the living room, his butt no match for Bob's. No surprise. When he dropped the phone on the bed, it stopped ringing, but I checked and it was from my home number—Alyssa. I called right back.

I heard her little girl's voice, both sad and scared. "Mom. I thought you'd be home by now. I need a cigarette but there was a weird guy down there again. Can you come with me?"

I told her I'd be home in a few minutes. Such an odd request, to accompany her to smoke. I would let her pollute my porch when I got back.

"I'm sorry. Gotta go. At least the call didn't, ah, interrupt..."

Leo laughed. "At least! Damn it, I wish you could stay the night."

"That's a song by one of my favorite singers, 'Stay the Night.'"

"Jane Oliver. One of my favorites, too."

I retrieved my clothes and hiked into the bathroom to deodorize. I did not want to go home smelling of sex, although my face was a giveaway—my lips looked collagen-injected and my cheeks looked like a rouge pot had been emptied on them. My mind was having trouble fitting Alyssa in—it only had room for Leo. He was the embodiment of loving kindness to me.

When I emerged, Leo had his yoga pants on with an old sweatshirt. He grabbed me into a long kiss. "I love you, Irish. Now get out."

When I walked into my porch, Alyssa was sitting in the dim light, her mouth open and her head hanging down. She barely acknowledged my presence. "Al, honey. You can have your cigarette here on the porch whenever it's dark outside or 'weird' guys are around. Okay?"

"Uh-huh." She let a minute pass, then turned toward me. "So you and old Leo been doing it?"

"Wh-what a question! It doesn't deserve an answer."

She ran into the house and came back with cigarettes and a Coke can for ashes. She lit up, ignoring me as I stood like a statue on the porch. Finally, after a few drags, she asked, "You look like you want one. Take." She handed over the pack of Camel Lights.

Oh, how I wanted that cigarette. "No thanks. I smoked years ago, and it took too much effort to stop. Not worth starting up again."

"Dad used to smoke sometimes at the work site. Did you know that?"

"He told me—and I smelled it. He said it was only occasionally, and mostly with his workers who were on break."

"Yeah. Guys who worked for Dad really liked him. Remember how I spent a few high school vacations on the job with Dad?"

"I remember. You had fun. So did your father."

She started to heave with muzzled sobs. "Why'd he have to die so young? It's not fair." She stubbed out her cigarette, gasped a few times, then lit another. "I hate, hate, hate that he's not here. And that it took him so long to die!"

"He had good times during those years. It was only the last year that was—"

"Don't talk about it. He must have hated me. I was never there. I was..." Again, stifled crying consumed her.

"He always loved you, Alyssa. Always."

"Leave me alone...please." She assumed the fetal position in the big chair. I went inside, wishing I could smoke a whole pack of cigarettes. Instead, I went straight to bed with Miles Davis's *Kind of Blue* blowing at me. Miles, I hoped, would alleviate my worry and pain.

Chapter 23

I woke sore enough to know I should visit my gynecologist since I had become a sexually active senior. That had a pathetic ring to it—life in a sixty-nine-year-old's fast lane. It was Sunday and I wanted to go to church, but I didn't want to leave depressed Alyssa alone. I sat on a stool at the kitchen counter, eating oatmeal buried in maple syrup to make it palatable, when Al showed up in sweat pants and an old T-shirt.

"Hey. You want some oatmeal? There's more."

"Ugh. No. Thanks. I'm gonna grab coffee and go down for a smoke."

"Stay on the porch for your smoke. And I'd really like it if you'd come to my UU service today. The minister is great and they always have good music. Okay?"

"I can't sit in one place that long. I'll just stay here and do email and Internet research. Go. I feel like mama bear's watching over me."

"Okay. I'll have my phone if—"

"I won't need to call you. Just go."

It took me twenty minutes to get myself showered and groomed, and I noted that Alyssa was on the porch with coffee and computer. "Smoke on the porch while I'm gone. Be back in two hours." Was I afraid she'd run away or be kidnapped? I knew I wanted her to stay in the apartment.

"Don't rush. I'll take you up on staying up here to smoke."

***

A substitute minister led the service—a handsome forty-something man with a sincere and caring demeanor. A natural for ministry. He talked about love and the need to be open and vulnerable to receive love. He said we often put up barriers to protect ourselves from being hurt and, in doing so, keep others from knowing us and loving us. The sermon resonated with me—I did not want to lose a loved one again. Was I afraid of letting myself love Leo? Afraid of letting him become too important to me?

We sang one of my favorite UU hymns, "Come Sing a Song." Afterward, my clique surrounded me during coffee hour, which was held outside in the garden on such a perfect day. We stood under a tree filled with purple flowers, the sun painting tree shadows all around us.

Sylvia asked, "How are things going with your daughter?"

I hadn't been to church in two weeks and had told no one about my trip to New York. "Alyssa is back with me. And she's working hard to get better—I think, hope."

Sylvia gave me a quick hug. "Make sure you take care of yourself too, dear."

"Thanks. I'm living in the moment, for sure."

Millie patted me on the back. "Call on any of us if you need help, you hear? Get your daughter to come to services. We'll all welcome her."

I rolled my eyes and laughed. "Tried that this morning. But, if at first...and all that jazz."

I extricated myself from the coffee klatch and drove home enveloped in the warmth and love from my friends, from the service music, from the beauty of our little church's garden—the sweet scents of the fecund jungle growth of early May in Florida. Maybe I could convince Alyssa to come with me the next week. She had loved our New Jersey UU church and went to religious education classes there for many years. For once I was filled with optimism, not my usual black Irish mood.

***

It was noon when I walked into my living room and there was no sign of my daughter. "Alyssa," I called, then yelled even louder, "Alyssa!"

My worry gene shifted into overdrive and acid reflux replaced my church afterglow. I opened her bedroom door a crack and peeked inside. The bed was barely visible under a suitcase, a computer, and a mound of dirty clothes. Damn. She must have gone outside to smoke again. I knew she'd smoked a few on the porch because I smelled the dead cigarette stench when I walked in and found butts left in a cup. I'd already flushed them down the toilet.

Lunch. Maybe some Tums followed by food would settle the growing fire in my throat. I'd taken my Prilosec that morning. Hadn't I? I hated to take an extra—Susan told me Prilosec might damage my bones. Everything in life has side effects—why aren't more of them good?

My landline rang. I heard "Call from Susan" from its computer-generated voice. Maybe Al was with her aunt. I snatched up the phone. "Sue. Is Alyssa with you?"

"Listen up! That's why I'm calling. Got a strange call from Alyssa a couple of hours ago—I just picked it up. Wanted to tell me she loved me and hoped I'd always take care of her mother. I'm out of town—"

"Oh, oh, God...she's missing." I took a breath. "Well, maybe just smoking or walking or—"

"Go look for her! I'll come over as soon as I get home. You call me when you find her, okay?" Susan's cell went dead.

Where would I search first? I ran out of the apartment and took the stairs three at a time, almost stumbling down the last few. I trotted over to the smoking area—two benches hidden under a canopy with one of those tall skinny containers that eats cigarette butts standing nearby. One of our more ancient residents sat puffing away. He looked up with that furtive "you've caught me being naughty" look crossing his face.

"Have you seen my daughter, Alyssa?"

He knew her since they were both regulars. "Nope. Haven't laid eyes on the pretty girl."

I thanked him and jogged over to the pool. I could feel the beginnings of an anxiety attack whipping up my heartbeat. I looked over the fence, scanning the few people there. Leo saw me, waved, and walked over.

He was smiling as he approached, but the look of adoration on his face changed to concern when he got closer. "What's wrong? You're white as a sheet."

"Alyssa disappeared while I was at church. She called Susan and asked her to 'take care of her mother.'"

"You search your condo?"

"Well. Peeked into her room—"

"I mean, really search."

"Well, no...I yelled her name—"

"I'll come with you. Let me grab my shoes."

We took the elevator. Leo squeezed my hand. "She probably just took a long walk. Let's see what's missing from her things, like her phone, or wallet, or cigarettes. That'll give us a clue."

We marched straight into her room; the mess was so widespread I didn't know how to determine what might be missing. Leo opened her bathroom door and emitted a low yowl. "Don't come in! Call 911. Stat!"

Not heeding Leo's order, I ran toward the bathroom. He blocked the door, "Get out! Call now!"

I got a glimpse of Alyssa, her white body in the tub, bloodied pink water up to her breasts.

I didn't scream or cry, just ran into the living room and grabbed the phone. I was shaking so hard I could barely tap those three numbers.

"911. What is your emergency?"

Through lips suddenly dry and parched, I stammered, "My daughter tried to kill herself. Blood. In tub." Between sobs, hiccups, and rapidly-escalating breathing, I answered their endless questions. *Fuck, no panic attack now.*

Carrying the phone with me, I sprinted back to the bathroom. Leo had Alyssa's body on the floor and was performing mouth-to-mouth resuscitation. She was a ghost, white and naked on the brown tile floor with Leo kneeling over her. He shifted to pressing on her chest.

I could not take my eyes off them. "What can I do?" My heart hammered in my chest, a trapped tiger trying to escape. I heard her cough and saw her eyelids flutter. I fell on my knees. "Alyssa, my baby girl. Oh, my baby…"

"Get me some gauze or strips of cloth to wrap her cuts." He'd elevated her wrists by wrapping them in her bathrobe and connecting the belt to the toilet seat. It looked like a horrific rape scene from a Tarantino film.

I hurried to my bathroom, jerked open the linen closet, and pawed through the toiletries searching for gauze, tossing things helter-skelter until I found it.

I returned with the gauze and noticed Alyssa's color looked better—surely a good sign.

Leo looked up at me. "She's breathing on her own now. Get a blanket. She's in shock. I need to cover her."

I flew out again. When I returned with the blanket and a pillow, I cautiously took a closer look at her.

Unintelligible mumbling came from her barely-moving lips. *Thank God, she's alive.* My knees hit the tile and my head fell down. Images of Alyssa at every age flickered like an old movie in my head—her bald head nursing at my breast, a toddler on her dad's shoulder, kicking a soccer ball in grade school, walking down the aisle for her high school graduation. And now.

Leo wrapped one wrist with gauze and started on the second. He was a skilled doctor, doing everything in rapid but perfect movements, his concentration zeroed in on Alyssa. He wisely kept me busy, maybe staving off another of my attacks.

"Wait by the door so the EMTs can get right in. She's alive but she needs a hospital. Call Ben. Let him know what happened. Now, get out of here."

I went out into the open corridor in time to hear the sirens of the ambulance coming into the entrance. The wailing stopped abruptly when they reached the building entrance. I dialed Ben's number and left a message with his answering service. By then the EMTs had arrived; a woman and a man exited the elevator and jogged toward me, the tall guy pushing a gurney, the young woman carrying a medical bag.

"This way," I called, motioning them to follow.

We headed toward the bathroom. Leo had wrapped Alyssa in the blanket and had the pillow under her head. I saw bloody water draining from the tub.

He again ordered me to leave the area. "Let the EMTs do their job."

I could hear them talking softly as I sat on Alyssa's bed, dizzy, my breathing ragged. I put my head between my legs and talked out loud to myself: "You're good in an emergency. Keep yourself together."

It took them only a few minutes to strap Alyssa's blanket-wrapped body to the gurney and wheel her to the door. I looked from Leo to the emergency crew. "I'm coming in the ambulance with her. Okay?"

Leo answered. "We'll both go. Grab your purse. We'll take the stairs. Are you able to walk down? You look wobbly."

"I'll make it. Just stay with me."

Leo watched me as I gathered my things, probably evaluating my level of breakdown. I held the railing as we hurried down the stairs.

"It could've been much worse," Leo said softly. "She missed the arteries and the second cut wasn't that deep."

We caught up with the paramedics as they hoisted Alyssa inside. Alyssa's old smoking buddy and several folks from the pool stood gaping at us. No one said a word. Soon we were off with sirens blaring, déjà vu for me, except I was a passenger and not the patient. I saw Susan's car pull into the parking area as we blazed out.

***

At the hospital, Leo gripped my hand as we followed Alyssa's progress to a curtained ER room. Leo's skin was as white as his hair. Pings and bongs, public address system calls to doctors, voices and cries—all bombarded us; the ER was a madhouse to the uninitiated. I let Leo answer most of the questions in doctor-speak. Of all people, sour Dr. Jonas, Bob's ER buddy, was the physician. After talking to Leo, she asked me if I knew Alyssa's blood type. I told her O positive, and I was positive because she'd needed a transfusion after a childhood accident.

Dr. Jonas barely glanced at me as she said, "We'll type her anyway. She's lost a lot of blood. Are you O positive too?"

"No, I'm—"

"Okay then, I'll get her started on a transfusion." With that brisk statement, Dr. Jennifer Jonas turned and marched away. I had questions, but she was as compassionate as a hyena.

At last, I could touch my daughter. I took her hand and began rubbing it. "I love you, Alyssa. We'll make things better, you and me. I promise."

She was silent those first few minutes, but big tears leaked from her eyes and slid toward her ears. Then I heard her say, "Sorry. You shoulda let me go."

I kissed her forehead. "I love you and I need you."

"No one needs me. I'm worthless. I'm…" Her voice trailed off.

"I need you. Hang in there. Please."

The next person to enter the roomette was Bob—there I was in his ER again. He looked over at Leo, then at me. "I'm the nurse supervisor today. I just glanced at the intake and saw Alyssa's name. I'll keep on top of her case. Don't worry."

At Alyssa's bedside he said, "Hey, Alyssa. It's Bob. You tell me if you need anything. If you want privacy, I'll throw them all out. Can you talk?"

A peep of "Yes" came out of her mouth.

An aide came in with a bag of blood; apparently Dr. Jonas trusted my knowledge after all. Bob hung the bag on a chrome pole and turned to us. "Could you step out, please? I need to move around."

I peered in through the edge of the curtain. He began by putting in an IV line and starting the blood flowing into her vein. Then he hooked her up to all the electronic paraphernalia, talking to her as he worked, explaining every step he was taking, his voice soft music, a lullaby. We watched the monitor: her heartbeat spiking on the screen, her blood pressure and oxygen levels fluctuating numbers.

We heard Bob say to her, "You'll have to stay here under observation in the psych ward for at least seventy-two hours. I'll make sure you get the Suboxone you need. I've contacted Dr. Ben and Dr. Whiting. They're both coming in."

When she heard Dr. Whiting's name, she winced and said, "Not her. I don't want to see her."

"I'll ask Ben if he can find another shrink, but for now will you talk to her? Okay? I've heard only good things about Whiting, honestly."

"Whatever, I guess. I'm an inmate now."

Bob was holding Alyssa's hand and leaning over her as he spoke. "I'll check on you a few times every day. You gotta get better, Suzanne!" He rolled himself away from her bed, dropping his head down. "Ah, sorry, Alyssa." After his faux pas, Bob looked up at me, and pain passed over his face. He shrugged.

Alyssa was alert enough to ask, "Who's Suzanne?"

We all heard him answer. "My daughter. She died in a car accident. You remind me of her. So you better get better. You hear?" He walked over to us. "I'll check in every few minutes." He looked us up and down, shook his head, and said, "You both look like hell. Go get something to eat."

I realized it was after three and I'd had no lunch. A dizzy spell rocked me, and Leo took my arm to hold me up.

"We'll be back soon. I'm taking her to the cafeteria. We both need food."

Poor Leo had arrived in just a bathing suit and a shirt. Bob handed him a doctor's white coat. It looked goofy with his skinny legs exposed. Bob looked so young and vigorous, with his dark hair and prizefighter's body, while Leo appeared so old and vulnerable, caught in the cool air conditioning without warm clothes.

We picked up pizza, salad, pie, water, and large cups of hot tea. We hardly spoke the first few minutes as we stuffed food into our hungry bodies. Leo had expended huge amounts of energy with his rescue earlier and he ate like a hungry bear.

I took Leo's hands. "You are a wonderful doctor! You saved Alyssa's life. I...I..." Tears stifled my voice.

"Don't go all maudlin on me. Any doctor would have done the same thing."

"So not true. You were amazing, and you knew to order me out and about too."

"Well, I didn't want two patients." He smiled and squeezed my hands. "You've been holding up well."

"I'll break down completely when I know everything is under control. So expect another patient soon."

"I'd like this patient to spend the night with me—no sex, no pressure—so I can hold you close and know you're okay."

"I've never had a better offer."

When we got back to the ER, Alyssa was sleeping soundly. Bob came in and said, "She's been given a mild sedative and will sleep a while." He called a young nurse over. "This is Liz. She'll drive you home. Get some rest. Alyssa will be in a room by evening, on the psych corridor. You can visit from 6:00 to 8:00 tonight."

***

Leo and I separated at the Gardens to rest and recover. The plan was for me to go back by myself to visit Alyssa in the evening and join Leo when I returned. I had called Susan from the hospital and filled her in. She said she'd meet me at home and would take care of "things" at my apartment before I got back. Susan had been helping me through all my life crises since we met our freshman year at NYU. Of course, I'd do anything for her too, but she always seemed to be in control of her life—except for her overeating, which probably started in the womb.

When the elevator doors opened on my floor, I wanted to crawl down my corridor to get to my condo door, but managed to remain upright. Susan was waiting on the porch and she jumped up to open the door and give me a huge hug. She made snorting sounds and said, "*Bubala*, go take a hot shower. You stink! Brought you some chicken soup. I'll stay until you've eaten some."

"Thanks. You're a dear. And I'll be out of the shower in a jiff."

After the hot shower and hot soup, it was after six, so I sent Susan off and drove my drowsy self to the hospital. I played a jazz album at high volume to keep from falling asleep at the wheel—I probably wouldn't have been able to hear a siren or horn, even from a fire engine. At the hospital, I got directions to Alyssa's room. The corridor was locked and I needed a special pass to go in. I found her sitting up in bed with an untouched tray of dinner in front of her—and no more blood bag flowing into her body, just a clear IV fluid.

"Hi. Can I come in?"

"Yeah. Welcome to my incarceration." Her voice was crackling, like an old hen. "Is *he* still with you?"

"If you mean Leo, no. He's exhausted. He saved your life. Heroically, I might add."

"It's too weird. Just, ah, not ready to face him yet. Didn't want saving, but, y'know, well, feeling kinda stupid now. But better. Really!"

She continued to babble. I interrupted. "I brought you some of Aunt Susan's chicken soup. It's still hot. And some clothes too."

She must have been feeling better since she scarfed down the bowl of soup in a few minutes and said thank you.

"Bob came in and talked to me about his daughter. So sad. He cried. Me too." She blew her nose and coughed up something green. "He's a great guy and a good nurse. Shoulda been a doctor or a shrink. I wish he was my shrink."

"I think he is, in a way. And another rescuer."

"And Dr. Whiting came too. Ah, well, she was better today. Not so pushy. Didn't try to make me talk about stuff. And Ben came for a few minutes. He'll be back tomorrow. I guess I'm getting VIP treatment 'cause of Leo and Bob." She looked almost happy for a moment. "And because of you. They're all your friends."

"I know Bob would like to be your friend, Al. And Ben too. And Leo."

"Doubt that. After my comments that night." The almost-happy moment had passed, and she turned her head toward the window. "Ah, can you go now? I need to be alone."

I leaned over and kissed her forehead and removed her tray. "Good night. Love you."

I got lost trying to get out of the hospital and had to ask three people for directions to my parking area. When I clicked off my Prius at home, I had no memory of driving at all. I would not tell Leo.

***

I rang his doorbell at 7:30, and he opened the door instantly and swept me into a tight embrace. "Sweetheart. What an awful day. How's Alyssa?"

"She seems to have made some emotional and physical progress, or I hope so. I don't want to be too optimistic. I think having Ben and Bob as her support group has helped."

"Sit. Sit." He took my big sack, which had overnight necessities in it. "You look like one drink and you'll fall asleep on the sofa."

"Close. One small drink. And something sweet. I'm craving sweets suddenly."

"Got key lime pie. That go with limoncello?"

"Goes perfectly. Big piece, please." I tried to get up and follow him into the kitchen, but he insisted I stay seated. He had the album we'd recently discussed and the plaintive tones of Jane Oliver singing "Stay the Night" added to my melancholy. "How about that jazz album you bought? Jane's idea of staying the night is too gloomy."

"Your wish is my command. How 'bout Wynton Marsalis, okay?"

"Perfect." Shortly, Wynton's trumpet filled the room and picked up my spirits, as did the tart-sweet pie and chilled drink.

I slipped my shoes off and curled up next to Leo, ready to nod off.

"If you put your feet in my lap, I'll give you a great foot massage."

The offer instantly brought back memories of John. He used to massage my feet whenever we watched TV together, and it always relaxed me more than five Valium could. I turned around and offered my feet to Leo. He pulled them into his lap and manipulated them with his skilled doctor's hands, sending relaxing waves throughout my body, the tingles hitting the top of my head.

"Wow. You could have a whole new career as a reflexologist or...relax-ologist. Ahh." After ten minutes of ultimate bliss, accompanied by groans and sighs, I said, "I'm feeling selfish here. You're spoiling me."

"Exactly what I had in mind. So you'll come back for more!"

"It's only about, what, nine, but I'm fading. Let me get my PJs on and you'll get to see me without any makeup."

"I've seen you in worse conditions. No threat there, hon."

I came back to the sofa wearing soft PJ bottoms with a matching blue T-shirt, having scrubbed and brushed. He had changed into blue tailored pajamas and his eyes followed me as I walked in. He patted the sofa next to him. "Sit. Let's talk a minute before sleep."

I sat.

"You know Alyssa will probably need a good rehab? And Ben wants to help."

"Yeah. I thought about that. And I know he knows about this stuff."

"Is it okay if I have Ben try to convince her to go?"

"More than okay. I hope he can."

"And you'll notice I'm keeping my promise—no taking advantage of you tonight. Let's go to bed and just spoon, okay?"

It was the second time that night I was ambushed by thoughts of John, who loved to spoon in bed. A warm glow climbed up my body that somehow allowed me to feel cherished by both men. I grinned up at Leo and gave him my hand. "Yeah, let's spoon away."

Chapter 24

Leo spoiled me the next morning with almond croissants from a local French bakery (he'd gotten up at dawn to run out) and cappuccino from his impressive machine. I'd slept better than I had in the last month—spooning must have released my melatonin reserves, although I escaped his spoon as soon as he fell asleep. Feelings of hope about Alyssa were percolating in me also—she was in good hands with Ben and Bob. Leo and I were, for some reason, rather bashful with each other that post-spooning morning. Spending the night with someone leaves you vulnerable, whether you had sex or spoons. We were suddenly more of a couple—the commitment level had been notched up.

The psych ward visiting hours would start at ten, so I went home to call Susan and change. She'd asked me to take her to visit Alyssa. We arrived at Al's room and knocked on the open door.

Alyssa was sitting in a chair, dressed in the jeans and the shirt I'd brought in the night before. Her hair was combed; she still looked anorexic, but healthier than yesterday. We took turns giving her a peck on the cheek, then I sat on her bed and Susan pulled up a chair. I finally noticed how much weight Sue had lost and felt insensitive for not having congratulated her. I made a mental note to compliment her later.

Susan lost no time. "You listen up, Al. You're the closest thing I got to a daughter, so you gotta get help. These two old broads need you."

"I'm trying, honest. Ben was in, y'know, Dr. Ben; we're talking about...stuff."

It hurt me she could talk to Ben and not to me, but at least I knew she was letting someone help her. Susan, of course, did not know about Ben's past addictions, but I assumed he was sharing that with Alyssa. I cleared my throat to get Al's attention. "So, what can we get for you? You want us to come back with a Chinese dinner tonight—all your favorites?"

"Yeah. Okay." Her voice was flat and she still would not look me in the eyes. She looked over at Susan though. "Auntie Sue, you...well, you're looking good. What're you up to, huh?"

Sue grinned ear-to-ear. "Well, you're more observant than your mother here. Lost close to forty pounds the past few months. And, you won't believe, I'm gettin' married in a couple of months." She shook her index finger at Alyssa. "You better be at my wedding."

Alyssa smiled for the first time in weeks, or months maybe. "I'll be there. Love you, y'know."

Oh, how I wanted her to tell me those words—I was now jealous of Ben *and* Susan. *Patience.* We chatted a few more minutes until

Alyssa asked us to let her rest. We'd return that evening bearing those little white takeout boxes.

My cell went off as we were leaving the hospital. It was Ben—I really did not know him well, but he seemed almost like family. Certainly my growing bond with Leo, and Ben's involvement with Alyssa, had jump-started our relationship. Like his father, he appeared to be a very concerned physician, and he and Al had formed a bond. Was it because of shared addiction problems or something more?

"Hi, Maureen. I know the ideal rehab for Alyssa. Good psychiatric care for her, ah, possible bipolar, and top reputation. Nice place, pool, a lake. They have an opening—it's pricey. Do you want me to help get Alyssa in?"

"Yes. Sure. What's the name of it? I'll research it online."

"Twin Lakes Health Center, west of Delray Beach. I know it well, Maureen, having spent two months there."

"I don't know how I'll ever thank you—or your father, the rescuer."

"He's pretty amazing for seventy-five, huh?"

"For any age!"

After I spoke to Ben, I noticed Susan staring at me with her question-mark face. She said, "So. Let's go to the Goddess and have lunch. I've missed you."

In the towering lobby of the hospital, she held out her arms and we embraced, a strong and long hug. People hurrying by paused to stare—we didn't care. When we came apart, I said, "You do look fabulous. It's not that I didn't notice. Sorry…"

"Hey. No worries. I understand. Our girl needs you, needs us. What does Hilary say—'It takes a village…'?"

***

We drove to the Goddess and poured our hearts out over cappuccinos and maple-walnut scones. Susan and Michael had finally done "it" and she was exuberant, albeit overly explicit. I did not want to know even one more detail about her K-Y Warming Jelly use.

"Susan, dear, I'm happy for you in every way. Let's avoid the details, okay?"

"You the rhymin' prude now?" She giggled and shook her finger at me. "I decided to visit a gynecologist before Michael and I attempted anything, me being a hundred years out of practice, and she had me talk to her PA for an hour. Gal gave me pamphlets to read, an estrogen cream, and the jelly stuff. You want her name?"

"No. I'm…functioning."

"Oh? You and Leo *shtupping* now?"

"Susan! Enough." I had to laugh—my first guffaw in ages. I laughed until tears ran out—tears of amusement for a change. "But, yes, we are…well, we did."

Susan's loud, hyena laugh always attracted an audience. To outsiders, we appeared to not have a care in the world. Sue said, "Back to our gal. If this Ben can get her into rehab, that'll be super, and I'll help you pay."

"I can pay. No problem there. If money could cure this, I'd give up everything."

"You can only do what you can do. Then it's up to her to learn to love herself again."

"Oh, Sue. I wish she'd learn to love me again."

"She loves you, hon. She just knows how much she's hurt you. Hang in there."

***

We arrived at Alyssa's room for supper carrying leaky bags of moo shu pork, ginger chicken, fried noodles and vegetables, but no fortune cookies—I made sure they were left out. Cheerful platitudes and silly advice might depress Alyssa—or me. I knocked and we found Alyssa deep in conversation with Ben.

"Mom, Aunt Sue, hi. Ben, this is my mom's best friend, Susan Katz. Aunt Sue, Dr. Ben Silverman." She grinned. "I believe you know his father."

Susan ducked in and shook Ben's hand. "I hear you're taking good care of our gal, Doctor."

He smiled up at Susan. "I'm trying. And please call me Ben."

"Okay. You want to stay for Chinese with us?"

"Smells great, but I have to run." He leaned down and patted Alyssa's hand, but I was in a position to notice the look of affection, or deep caring, on his face. Well, I would ask Leo what he thought about that.

Looking around at us three women, Ben backed out the door saying, "Bye now. Enjoy dinner." His voice betrayed a bit of discomfort.

Susan and I placed all the boxes on the bed and I served everyone on paper plates as we sat around a tiny tray table, large enough to hold our cups of tea. Susan said, "Okay. Gotta stick with tradition here. A Chinese man says to a Jewish guy, 'Our culture goes back four thousand years.' Jewish guy responds, 'Well, ours goes back over five thousand!' Chinese man says, 'Not possible. Where did you eat for those thousand years?'"

"Aunt Sue, you're...you're amazing. You must know a million jokes."

"Well, life in the fat lane. I had to be funny."

Alyssa and I both started to talk. I let Alyssa have the floor. "You're the smartest lady, and the nicest, and the most loyal, and...Mom and me, we're lucky to have you, y'know."

Susan grinned and said, "Thanks, but I'm the lucky one. You're my family!" Sue then waved her left hand up and down in front of us. "Observe. At age seventy, I have my first engagement ring."

A huge diamond glittered in the fluorescent hospital light. I sputtered, "Wow...wow. It's...it's stunning, lovely." *And huge.*

Susan's high-decibel laughter filled the room. "I told him not to waste his money and he said, 'So, I should take it with me. I want you to have the world's most gorgeous ring.' I stopped saying no."

When we finished eating and schmoozing, Susan said what I wanted to say. "Alyssa, about the rehab business. You ready for that?"

Al nodded her head. "I've made such a mess, of everything, but this…thing in the bathtub…it woke me up. And, I was gonna tell you both tonight. Day after tomorrow, Ben'll drive me to Twin Lakes." She paused and patted my hand. "Is that okay with you, Mom?"

I blinked back the beginnings of tears but said, "I think it's a great idea. I'd love to drive you there, but if, well, you know, if you'd rather—"

"Mom, Mom. Ben, he's really helping me. And he knows the director. And it's less emotional, for me, for us, if he does."

I felt happy she was going to rehab, sure, but miserable that she preferred going with Ben. Between my years of mourning and her corresponding years of addictions, our relationship needed rebuilding, that was obvious. But how? Patience, I told myself, or *ksanti*, as Anika called it in yoga classes. Never a virtue I could call mine, but I would keep trying.

In a voice I hardly recognized as my own, I said, "Al, remember I want to help you any way I can. I might need a little help directing myself, so—"

Alyssa looked right at me for a change. "Mom. I know what you've already done. I know I never said thank you for being the bravest mom who ever lived, y'know, coming to Brooklyn that day. I…I think…"

Alyssa choked back tears. I got up and gave her a lopsided hug. "You just get better. That's all I'll ever want."

***

That night I tossed and turned, wandered around my condo in my nightwear, took a hot bath around two in the morning, then, after all else failed, swallowed a Valium and slept. Alyssa's addiction to opiates made me worry about my reliance on Valium to relax and to sleep. I was positive I didn't take it too often, but it still worried me. I'd talk to my physician about it soon. It was not something I wanted to discuss with Leo.

Leo. He'd wanted another "sleepover," but I told him I needed to be alone. He responded as though I'd told him to go sleep with pythons in the Everglades. I was thrilled for Susan that she'd committed herself to Michael. After a lifetime living alone, she was going to move into his home, the one furnished by his dead wife. The thought of Susan moving away frightened me. I envied her, but I was already feeling suffocated by Leo. Why? Why couldn't I give up some privacy for a loving partner? *Ksanti*. Everything required patience.

I needed a good talk therapist to help me figure out my plans for the rest of my life. And to help me deal with my new sexual awakening. And to talk to me about Alyssa's rehabilitation. And to help me understand why I was terrified by Leo's love. I'd gone from hiding inside a cocoon of bereavement to feeling like Lady Godiva without the long hair.

I kept busy laundering Alyssa's clothes, packing a suitcase for her to take to Twin Lakes, cleaning my messy apartment, catching up on mail and email. Most of Alyssa's clothes would start out too big, but she was gaining weight. Leo called after I'd had lunch. I was resting, feet up, on the porch.

"Sweetheart, how are you? Can you come over for dinner tonight? Ben's coming and he'd like to talk to us."

"I'm too tired. Couldn't sleep. How about I come over right after dinner, for a nightcap? Okay?"

"Hmm. A stay-the-nightcap, maybe?"

"No. Too drained."

I agreed to meet them at 7:30 for dessert. Leo again sounded wounded. *Damn.*

***

Of course, even though I was afraid of romantic attachment, I was exhausted, and, and...I still had to fix my hair, my makeup, and dress for maximum femininity. Susan said I'd gotten too much out of life because of my looks, so I now tried too hard to maintain the unattainable—that old fountain of youth. How did she get so smart? She knew me too well—perhaps better than I knew myself.

At Leo's, Ben answered the door and gave me welcoming air kisses. Leo came out of the kitchen carrying a tray of pear tarts from a local French bakery. He remembered I'd said I loved them weeks ago. So damned solicitous!

We sat outside on his lanai, one of the loveliest places to be: fountain, jasmine, lake, birds, love in bloom. What was wrong with me that I wanted to run?

Ben said, "Maureen. I've got paperwork for you to fill out. Do you have any questions about Twin Lakes?"

"Yes. Lots. When can I visit? And how often? And how do I pay? And—"

"Sorry. I forgot you're not as familiar with the place as we are. I've got a brochure for you with all that info. And they have a special section of their website for family members. I got you the password." He handed me a folder of papers, which I started to leaf through.

"I'll need the financial information filled out by tomorrow and a check for ten thousand. And I hope you don't mind me driving Alyssa. I offered, and she said she was afraid she'd cry all the way if you drove her. She knows how much she's hurt you, and herself. I think she'll be okay." He frowned. "Takes time; I know."

I was silent for a couple of uncomfortable minutes, then said, "Ben, thanks…I'll bring this all to the hospital tomorrow and leave it and her suitcase with Alyssa."

Ben got up, gave me a pat, hugged his dad, and left. Leo had been quiet all evening—annoyed because I hadn't come for dinner and was not planning a sleepover, I presumed. He cleared his throat a few times, his special preamble. "Just want you to know, I understand you need some time…to deal with everything. But call me if you need anything, okay?"

"I promise. When life quiets down, I'll cook dinner for you at my place. That's a big offer. I kinda gave up cooking a couple of years ago, but you've inspired me."

He walked over, pulled me up, and gave me a rock-the-baby hug, not a begging-for-sex hug. "I won't pressure you, but my bed is always available for any kind of sleepover."

"Good night, Leo the Lionhearted." I gave him a quick kiss and escaped.

Chapter 25

Brave me. I watched and waved as Ben drove off with Alyssa. I was smiling; I'd been smiling so much all morning—the upbeat mommy—my lips hurt. Now I could relax, maybe? She was safe. She was going to be in rehab for at least a month, probably two. No visitors were allowed the first week. So why couldn't I reduce my tension level? *Ksanti!* I mumbled the meditation, "I breathe in peace; I breathe out love."

I hadn't been to a yoga class in a week, so perhaps a return to routine might help. Tomorrow I planned to spend an hour and a half with Anika, whose yoga classes were specially designed to wring out tension.

When I got home, Leo called. No surprise. "Sweetheart, you've got a command performance! Jordy's team won the Florida state championship. He wants you to come to a celebration. This party is mostly for family. The team already had a blowout at that awful Chuck E. Cheese place."

It seemed like months ago when we danced at Jordy's bar mitzvah. I'd been living in tricky-time, my own theory of relativity: the higher your stress level, the slower time moves. "When is this party?"

"Sunday afternoon. Come down here about noon. Lunch will be huge—you know Marion, she loves to put on a spread." He performed his harrumph. "And...what about tonight? Dinner at a quiet waterfront restaurant?"

"Let's hold off till Sunday. I want to unwind, lie in the sun, do lots of yoga—"

"Then I'll drive us to yoga tomorrow—"

"No thanks. I'll see you there, but I'm meeting Susan after class, so..."

His voice seemed to lose its physician-confident tone. "Okay. See you Sunday. Call if you change your mind about dinner. Don't want you all alone."

"I'll call, but I need to be all alone for a while to recover. Gotta run. Bye."

***

Yoga helped—thankfully my flatulence was under control, and I felt rejuvenated by the end of class. Maybe that post-yoga glow was the fountain of self-healing. Leo had not shown up, so it was easier for me to clear my brain without his hovering over me. I didn't want to hurt his feelings; maybe I even loved him, but too much had happened too fast the past couple of months for me to process my own feelings. Alyssa's attempted suicide had machine-gunned out areas of my brain—pathways had been ripped apart. One casualty appeared to be my growing love for Leo. Was it merely that I felt guilty falling in love while my daughter's life was falling apart, guilty enjoying fine food and music, tender moments, while she shivered in withdrawal? Probably. Sylvia Boorstein, whose Buddhist meditation book I was still using, once said that a mother mortgages her heart when her child is born. Too much of my heart had been swallowed by Alyssa recently.

Also, I did not want to feel obligated to do the deed whenever Leo swallowed a blue pill. Lately I'd been thinking of intercourse as a form of combat. The male must penetrate the female, then proceed with violent thrusting to shoot off into her. Hmm. I needed to talk to Leo about his "staying power." Was it selfish of me? I enjoyed the buildup of sexual tension and the foreplay, but my insides were too old for the rest. Maybe I needed to pay a visit to Susan's doctor for a sex check-up and perhaps invest in some K-Y supplies. Why didn't Leo think about that stuff? His doctoring must never have included aging vaginas.

***

Susan had invited me to dinner to meet Michael Saturday night. With my life competing with the *Life of Pi*—Alyssa as the tiger in my raft—I'd never had time or energy to meet my best friend's intended. Susan was so calm, so self-assured, so in love. I always envied her matter-of-fact, accountant's way of dealing with life and emotions. Whenever I was angry with John or worried about Alyssa's high school antics, talking things over with Susan always calmed me down and made me laugh. She was a cross between Buddha and Joan Rivers—I hoped this Michael understood how lucky he was.

I knocked on Susan's door for our historic encounter. It felt a bit like going to meet the Pope—I certainly hoped I'd like him, since I knew I was stuck with him for the rest of our lives.

Michael answered her door. I stared longer than was polite—he was bald with a full-moon face, shorter than I, but adorable in a cherubic way. His smile was a happy face come to life. "Welcome, Maureen. I feel as though I've known you for years. Well, Susan does talk about you." He ended with an uncomfortable giggle, as though he'd revealed a secret.

I shook his soft, warm hand. He held on for an extra few seconds. "I'm so happy for both of you. You're marrying a queen, a *mensch*— what's female version of *mensch*?"

"I agree. She's a *mensch*. Come. Sit." He led me to the living room sofa.

Susan came out of the kitchen carrying a tray of hot puffy things. Normally, she spent less time in a kitchen than she did skiing in the Himalayas. She put the tray down as Michael opened a bottle of champagne with a resounding pop; the cork shot across the living room and pinged off Susan's TV screen.

Susan clapped her hands. "So. We're starting out with a bang. And celebrating you two finally meeting. The two most important people in my life!"

We clinked glasses and each uttered a loud *"L'chaim."* *To life* was an appropriate toast for a senior trio celebrating love and friendship.

I could feel the pressure of tears forming behind my eyes. "Michael. I hope to see a lot of you. Has Susan filled you in on my loony life?"

Michael moved his chair closer to me. "I hope you don't mind. She told me all about you rescuing your daughter in New York and, ah, everything that's happened since. I have an adult child with big problems, so I understand, a little, what you've been going through."

Susan sat next to me on the sofa as Michael beamed down on us. She took my hand and said, "Listen, Reenie, Michael and me, we want you in our life and maybe, when you're feelin' up to it, we'll all go out with Leo. You won't believe, but Michael and Leo know each other—both on the board of Sun Medical Center. It was only last week I learned this when I was tellin' Michael about how Leo, well, how he saved Alyssa."

Michael and I both started talking at once. I let him speak. "I can't believe it took so long for me to figure out who Leo was, but Susie didn't tell me his last name until last week. He's got a great reputation in the medical community."

I had to smile, both at the good Leo report and the "Susie." If I'd called her that, Susan would have poured her champagne over my head. I said, "I've watched Leo work. He is amazing."

We'd polished off the unidentifiable puffy snacks when a bell went off in the kitchen and Susan called us in to fill our plates. She'd made a lamb stew—I almost fainted with surprise. We sat at her dining room table where we usually had our Chinese takeout and Michael poured my favorite Pinot Noir into tall wine glasses.

Conversation was easy and fun. Michael and Susan were both tellers of tall tales and laughed at each other's stories. I liked Pope Michael.

When I got up to say goodbye, Michael gave me a hug and said, "I hope we'll be seeing you often…and, ah, hope I passed the test."

"What test?" I asked him.

"You know. The best friend passes judgment on the boyfriend."

"Well, if my opinion counts, and it shouldn't, you two seem made for each other. I will, by the way, be your maid-of-honor!"

I stumbled a bit walking to my elevator door—the champagne and red wine had banished any sad thoughts, but I must have looked like an old alcoholic heading home. Tomorrow I'd be greeting Jordy and enjoying the exuberance only a thirteen-year old could produce. And I'd avoided Leo for a couple of days—a healthy break, I thought. Like too much dessert, too much time together could upset one's equilibrium. Even slightly drunk, I felt more in control of my emotions than I had in ages.

Chapter 26

Sunday bloomed like a perfect rose opening and perfuming the air. I sat on my porch inhaling the sweet, salted air, the temperature a sweater-cool seventy, sipping my second cup of coffee. With Alyssa in rehab, I felt at ease for the first time since her arrival last month. I knew there was no permanent cure for addiction, but there was hope. Hope—I clung to that word, made it my mantra.

Nothing in my life had prepared me to deal with addictions and mental illness. Since I first learned of Alyssa's problems, I'd spent hours online reading article after article on bipolar disorder, and later, even more hours reading about opiate addiction. I even "hung out" at addiction chat rooms. *SkyHag claims this is her third time trying Suboxone to get off pills; rehab was a waste she says. SheLovesKoalas states that she made a mistake jumping off ½ mg. of Suboxone every other day. Icandothis does not want to use Suboxone to help withdraw from his Vicodin addiction. "I can do it cold turkey." Pookie says taking Suboxone saved her life. She was stealing to pay for her five-year-long Oxycontin addiction when her parents got her to a Suboxone doctor.*

At 11:30, I looked up from my comfy chair and was startled to see Leo standing outside my porch, studying me. "Sweetheart, you look like an angel. You ready?"

"I was daydreaming. Pleasantly, for a change." That was a lie, of course. Chat rooms had attacked my brain. I had forgotten the time but only needed to grab my purse. "Let's go."

Another top-down cruise to his son's house—the wind noise was so loud we couldn't talk. When we pulled into the driveway, Jordy ran down and opened my door. In his excited, octave-fluctuating voice he said, "Hey. You both missed my playoff game. And we won!"

As I walked up to the house with my thirteen-year-old boyfriend, I told him I'd been handling some difficult problems.

"I know. I heard you're like…super brave. I'm not supposed to know but I listen, so—"

"It's okay. I think you're old enough to understand, right?"

Jordy smiled at me. "Yeah, right."

Jordy's parents, Sam and Marion, and loud Aunt Bea, Leo's sister, descended on us. I received three big hugs as competing conversations ricocheted around me. I glanced over at Leo, hoping for a rescue, but he just laughed and shrugged. Jordy pulled me into the house. Some guests were sipping Bloody Marys and all looked familiar from the bar mitzvah, although I'd never remember their names. I was propelled into the den where Jordy's latest and greatest trophy was displayed. He picked it up reverently, handed it to me, then said, "I hope you're, like, part of the family now."

"Well, I guess I am, sort of. Your grandfather is my, my special friend. And congrats. This is an impressive trophy."

Leo interrupted. "Jordy. You're hogging my girlfriend again. Let's all go eat." Leo guided me to the patio where Sam was cooking burgers. Mountains of fancy salads were lined up on the table.

The next thirty minutes were consumed with serious plate loading, eating, and spirited talking. How did they all stay thin? I had Jordy on one side of me and Leo on the other—my protectors.

Leo had to talk into my ear for me to hear him over the din. "Let me know when you want to go."

Jordy jumped in. "I heard that, Grandpa. She can't go yet. I haven't introduced her to Friskie."

Sam added, "Friskie is our Goldendoodle puppy. He's in his crate, 'cause all this food and he'd drive us crazy."

"Then I'm staying to play with Friskie. I love dogs!"

That's all it took. Jordy had me out in the yard, running with Friskie, tossing Friskie a Frisbee. Tossing and tossing, over and over again, to the pup—six-months old, with long legs and curly-blonde hair, long floppy ears, and enough energy to run a marathon. And we tried to keep Friskie away from the patio where hamburgers still scented the air. I was glad I'd dressed in casual shoes and dark capris, because I ended up on the ground with Friskie on top of me, slurping my face, Jordy and Leo laughing hysterically.

Leo helped me up and I went inside to fix up. When I came out, Leo was saying goodbye and thank you to Marion, and I joined him. Marion said, "I think Leo wants you to himself. Anytime you'd like to go out for a quiet coffee someplace, please call me. I'll tell you the family secrets."

Jordy gave me a huge hug goodbye. "Come back soon, okay? Friskie wants to see you."

When we finally made it back to the car, Leo headed in the opposite direction from home.

"Where're we going?"

"Just wait."

We drove in silence, only the wind and traffic noise filling our ears. It was after two and the sun was too hot for me to enjoy having the convertible top down. Whenever we slowed for traffic or stopped for a light, I was self-basting with sweat. Fanning myself with a magazine I said, "Can we either put the top up or blast the air-conditioning? I'm melting."

At that moment, we pulled into a parking lot and Leo hit the button to put up the top. "We're here," he said, with an odd expression on his face. Fear, I thought, but why?

"Where's here?"

"It's my favorite park. Let's walk along the mangrove path, work off some of the calories from lunch."

We headed over to a path paved with wood-shavings and gravel. We were close to the ocean and a cool breeze chilled my sticky dampness. It was quiet—not another soul around. Almost too quiet for nervous me to be in a deserted wooded area. "Is it safe here?"

"Sure. Lots of fishermen all along this waterway. Look out there."

He was right. A few small boats were in the river with fishing rods hanging out over the water, fishermen languidly sitting back while slurping down cans of beer.

We reached a bench under a dense tree and Leo pulled me toward it. "Let's sit here a minute. I want to ask you, ah, something important."

We sat on the cool stone. He looked at me with his eyebrows knotted together, lips in a grimace. I panicked. "Did something happen to Alyssa? What's wrong?"

"This isn't working the way I'd hoped. Do I look like the bearer of bad news?"

I nodded yes.

"Damn. I want to ask you to marry me. Guess I'm afraid you'll say no." My face must have sent bad vibes back to him because he looked more stricken. "Don't say anything yet. I've got more to add." He held his hand up in front of me although I was speechless. "The condo next door to mine is for sale. I want to buy it for you—for us. I remembered you don't want to share a bathroom or have someone flailing around in bed. And I can convert the lanai and patio into one..." He took a breath.

He was holding my hand so tightly my circulation stopped. I pulled my hand away and shook it out. "Listen. I need to think, need more time."

His proposal, of course, probably wasn't the best time to bring up the gorilla sitting on my shoulder. But I had to do it soon or risk more pain. "Uh, there's an embarrassing problem we have to talk about.

Maybe this isn't the right timing. Damn. I'm—well, this isn't easy for me." I looked away, then got up and started walking.

Leo caught up with me. "Wait. What? Talk to me, please. I love you, you realize that, don't you?"

"I love you too. But—oh, how to say this—well, I'm still recovering from the sex we had—"

"What! Oh, no. Why didn't you say something? Tell me—"

"It's just that it took you so long to, uh, finish, it hurt. And maybe I still have some damage. I've got a doctor's appointment."

He threw his arms around me. "Oh, Maureen. Oh, God. We'll fix this. It's my fault. Over-medicated myself, ah, you know what I mean? Viagra, it works too well for me, but I wanted to be, to be young—for you. Damn." He was holding me and rocking back and forth. A young couple walked by us and gave backward glances accompanied by laughter. Maybe senior PDA is comedic.

We started walking back toward the car with Leo wringing his hands and kicking pebbles. "This is awful. Only wanted you to feel wonderful. Can I come with you to this doctor?"

"No! I can barely talk about any of this. I'm afraid my women's liberation did not include sexual liberation."

"You'll let me know what this doctor says, right? So, we can, uh, fix the problem."

The whole discussion suddenly hit my funny bone and I started to giggle, then bent over laughing so hard I couldn't breathe. When I looked up, Leo was covering his mouth trying not to guffaw. He finally let it out too. The same young couple passed us, this time whispering and looking back at our laugh-a-thon.

"Oh, Leo. I do love you. Everything else is secondary."

"And will you promise to be part of the rest of my life, one way or another?"

"I promise."

We were almost to the parking lot when Leo stopped to give me a warm, sloppy kiss, holding me close to his body, which was in ready position. I pushed him away. "Leo. I think this should wait for indoor time. We have an audience." The same couple plus two scantily clad teenage girls were watching us like we were the newest reality TV show—*Old Lovers from Lauderdale*. It would probably be a hit here in Florida.

***

On Monday I saw Susan's doctor and got the senior-sex talk—and lesson plans. According to the physician's assistant, it might be advantageous for me to bring Leo close to climax with my hands or mouth, then be on top where I could control the engine. I was sixty-nine and had never anticipated doing "69" or anything like it. My conservative Catholic upbringing had never allowed my mouth to travel below a navel. I was purple with embarrassment throughout the ordeal.

When I left, I was armed with two kinds of lubricants and two copies of a brochure titled "Senior Sexual Techniques." Who knew? It even had cute diagrams of sex with the woman on top, sex while facing each other on your sides—rather like the illustrated *Kama Sutra*

I'd snuck into my dorm room in 1962. Maybe I'd just slip the brochure under Leo's door—or run away and become a nun.

***

Alyssa's week of enforced isolation at rehab was over on Tuesday and she called me.

"Mom. Hi. Can you come out here for a visit soon?"

"Of course. When can I come?"

"Lunch on Saturday? It's a kinda visitor's day. No therapy sessions and stuff."

"I can't wait to see you. Can I bring you anything?"

"That old blue one-piece bathing suit if you can find it in my mess. And it had a matching cover-up. Bikinis aren't welcome here, and I've been swimming every day wearing someone's old tank. Being in the water clears my head."

"I'll find it. See you Saturday. Love you."

"Thanks, Mom, y'know, for everything."

I remembered the first line of an Alexander Pope poem: "Hope springs eternal in the human breast…" I felt hope bouncing around in my mortgaged heart.

***

I invited Leo to my condo for dinner on Wednesday—he'd begged me to go out but I felt it was time for me to cook for him. It would be his third time at my place—the first a brief, uncomfortable visit with Alyssa and Bob, the second his resurrection of Alyssa—and, hopefully, his first visit without obstacles.

I set out a bowl of wrinkled black olives and some nuts—Leo avoided the fatty cheeses I'd have been inclined to add. Two bottles of an expensive Pouilly-Fumé, my favorite white wine, chilled while I put a bouquet of freesia on the coffee table—we both loved the intoxicating scent. I seemed to wear a path in the carpet, pacing up and down my living room, beginning to dread what should be a lovely evening. I knew Leo would ask about my lady-doctor visit and I'd be uncomfortable talking about it. Later, he'd want to try out one of the brochure's techniques and, although I was healed, I was not ready to tackle tricky positions or...damn it. Senior sex was too fraught with frustration.

The female body is an amazing instrument with the right musician fingering, tonguing, and rubbing. Leo knew, without any instructions, how to start my engines, but I needed to shorten his crescendo. Pace, pace, pace. I was going bonkers. I put on a Wynton Marsalis CD, *J Mood*, a mellow, meditative jazz album, one I thought Leo might enjoy and one that usually relaxed me.

I answered Leo's ring at 5:30. He was early, but he was always a bit early—good training by his mother, he claimed. An orchid and a bottle of wine filled his arms, so whether to embrace or not was cleared up by gift placement. I put the orchid on the coffee table with the snacks. "Please, sit."

Leo beamed at me. "Not till I get a hug. I haven't seen you in a few days—missed you."

I really don't deserve this guy. I turned and gave him a hug, then dashed into the kitchen and brought out a bottle of wine in a cooler. "You pour, please."

I sat down in a rattan chair across from Leo, who was perched on my white sofa. He poured two glasses and handed me one. "Sweetheart. To the rest of our lives—together." We clinked glasses.

He was a romantic, no doubt. I loved that about him, but I was out of sync with his mood. I took a few sips of the cold, fruity wine. "I talked to Alyssa today. I'm visiting her on Saturday. She sounded okay." I tried to smile. "I'm still not sleeping, not without a Valium or a Benadryl. I can't stop the flashbacks of her in the bathtub."

"Hmm. I'm not happy with you taking meds to sleep. Once in a while is okay, but I think a talk with a therapist might help you. Or spending more time with me!"

"I'll think about both."

"Something smells wonderful. I know you hate to cook, so I feel honored."

A bell went off in the kitchen. "It's Chicken Marbella, every bad cook's favorite failsafe recipe."

A few minutes later I dished out the succulent chicken, added some jasmine rice, and we took our plates to my glass-topped dining room table. Somehow it felt too formal with only the two of us. Why was I so uncomfortable? We made "food talk" while eating, with Leo ladling on the compliments. By the time we sipped the last of the wine, the elephant in the room emerged.

"So, can you tell me about your doctor's sex advice?"

My stress had been gradually melting away—three glasses of wine can do that—but it ratcheted back up. "I'm not sure I can talk about it. They gave me brochures for each of us to read. I'm so shy about this...I...Can you just read it when you get home?" Between the wine and the embarrassment, I knew my cheeks were red-splotched and my ears a glowing red.

"Maureen, let me make a little speech, okay?"

I nodded.

"I love you, love taking rides with you, visiting family with you, eating with you, dancing, hugging, and, yeah, making love with you. But most of all, I want to be with you, near you, to know you've got my back, to help you, to know you'll be holding my hand when I'm dying. If we never have sex again, I'd still want you there all the time."

"I want to be with you too, including making love. I'm such a repressed old fool."

"You're one sexy dame. When I touch you, I feel your response. Don't worry so much."

I gave Leo the senior sex brochure to read and shooed him to the sofa while I cleaned up. Later, I brought two stemmed glasses of icy limoncello into the living room. Before I sat down, I put on Jane Oliver's *Stay the Night*. We sat next to each other on the sofa and I curled up against him as Jane's plaintive lyrics surrounded us.

"Can I take this as an invitation to stay here tonight?"

"Yes."

***

I slept soundly next to Leo—my first good rest since Alyssa's suicide attempt. Me, who did not want to share a bed. I woke at dawn and looked down at his sleeping body, curled into a fetal position, his bald spot shining in the pale light. Well, he didn't snore, nor flail, nor fart, at least not that I noticed. And he'd played my instrument *con amore* but said he'd had too much to drink and no Viagra, so there wouldn't be a finale. I think he was afraid to hurt me again because I felt his erection and used my hands (Lesson 1) to make him change his mind. The K-Y Warming Jelly (Lesson 2) was everything the brochure said and more. And the woman on top—yes, yes, yes.

I slipped out of bed, showered, fixed my face a bit, and put on a blue and white Japanese kimono from a vacation with John many years ago. When I stepped out of the bathroom, Leo was sitting up, his bare chest covered with curly gray hair. "You are beautiful. Get over here." I sat next to him on the edge of the bed and his arm wrapped around my waist. "Marry me, Irish. Okay?"

"Yes is the short answer. But, well, there's Alyssa. Don't know what's going to happen. And I want to wait till after Susan and Michael's wedding. It's in August and I want her to feel special."

"That's too long to wait. Let's elope and celebrate later."

"I can't keep a secret from Susan—I'd feel sneaky." I ran my hands over his furry chest and kissed him on his bald spot. "Leo, we don't need a ceremony to vow to be there for each other, do we?"

"I guess not. You have my vow."

***

I met Susan at the pool on Thursday afternoon and watched as she finished the last few minutes of her water aerobics class—what a transformation in my pal, who'd eschewed exercise her entire life. When she walked over and took a seat next to me, I grinned, filled with joy for her. "You look marvelous, dear."

"I know! I feel ten years younger, maybe twenty. Forty-two pounds lighter. Can you believe?" She started to laugh. "All those years you tried to get me to exercise. *Oy*, what took me so long?" Susan took my hand. "Enough about me. How you doin'? How's our gal?"

"I'm fine, with lots of help from Leo. And I'm visiting Alyssa on Saturday. She sounded good on the phone."

"You remind her my wedding's in August. Maybe you and Alyssa can both walk me down the aisle—my matron and maid of honor. I'm gonna make you wear an ugly pink dress like the one you put me in."

"Speaking of weddings." I paused. *Should I tell her?*

"Yeah?"

"Leo wants to marry me."

"Duh. Big surprise. First time I saw him lookin' at ya, I knew. He's so in love he looks loopy."

"Well, I told him we didn't have to get married, at least not right away, well, with Alyssa and all."

"Listen, Reenie. You take care of yourself first. Don't lose Leo. He's your rock."

"I know. But hey, you've been my rock my whole life."

"Don't get all weepy on me. I'll always be there too, just like you'll be there for me."

***

Leo and I ate together Thursday and Friday and I stayed the night at his condo on Thursday—no sex, but very loving. Since I was going to get an early start on Saturday for my visit with Alyssa, I spent the night alone at home and already missed him sleeping next to me. I did not need separate bedrooms—I slept better with Leo by my side. Maybe I'd still want my own bathroom.

I set my GPS and left at nine on Saturday, way too early, but I didn't want to risk missing the luncheon. My breakfast was heaving around, planning a return to the world, and my IBS was in overdrive, so maybe it was smart to have left early with time for extra bathroom stops. Why was I so nervous? Alyssa invited me. She was in the best facility possible. She was safe from drugs and, I assumed, watched for signs of depression. It should be the best visit we'd had in years: no drugs, no smartphones, no Darius, no clients. When I nailed it down, I was afraid she hated me—well, not hated, but I was sure she wished her father was alive and it was me who had died. She'd adored her father and avoided everything related to his illness. But, well, she was an adult—she had to fix herself. I kept *hope* sitting up front with me during the drive.

When I was almost there, I stopped at Dunkin' Donuts for a coffee to fill time, but spent the time in the bathroom. I needed my Imodium—stat. I located a CVS using an iPhone app and rushed in to purchase a bottle of my green liquid savior. I slugged some down like an addict.

I pulled into the Twin Lakes Health Center at noon. It looked like a vacation resort—a cluster of two-story Spanish-style buildings with red tile roofs and graceful archways. Royal palm trees lined the drive to the main building and parking. I'd no sooner stopped in the visitors' parking area when Alyssa appeared at my door.

What a transformation. She had a glowing tan. She was wearing a T-shirt and capris and her arms and legs were no longer sticks; her cheeks were pink and had some flesh—I wanted to pinch her face like I did when she was an infant.

I must have been frozen because I heard, "Mom. What are you waiting for? Get out of the car! I'll show you around."

I slowly got out of the car, feeling a little dizzy, a little short of breath. Seeing her looking so much better was a happy shock to my system. Standing up, I opened my arms and she fell into my embrace.

"Alyssa…you look…wonderful!"

"You look a whole lot better than last time I saw you too."

She actually took my arm—wow. Hope bubbled like a warm Coke on ice. We wandered on paths through lovely gardens. So far I hadn't seen another human.

"Mom, if I seem a little shaky, well, we're working on getting the right drugs into me and it'll take a while. But I love my shrink here—I can talk to him."

When we rounded a bend, I saw people eating outside on a patio, then spotted a buffet near the building's entrance. Four or five people waved or high-fived Alyssa as we headed toward the buffet.

"We can find a quiet table over by the fountain. Food's pretty good here."

Alyssa loaded her plate with salads and rolls and poured two tall, icy glasses of lemonade. I took very little and hoped my Imodium was still working. The woman behind the buffet smiled and said, "You must be Alyssa's mother. Welcome."

When we finally sat down at a table near the gushing fountain, I heaved out a sigh. "I'm so happy to see you looking so healthy. You have no idea how good it feels."

"I want to, I want you to know—shit, words are…Well. You, you are the bravest mom—in the world. In one of my groups I told them about you coming to that awful place in Brooklyn and confronting Shithead. They all said you're a hero. You are—my hero."

I felt tears of joy prickling my eyes. "Oh, Alyssa, oh…I love you."

Chapter 27

Alyssa spent two months at rehab and came out a different person—or, maybe, the person she would have been if her father hadn't died and addictions hadn't taken over her life. I watched her metamorphosis on my weekly visits to Twin Lakes. Each time I drove up that palm-lined drive, hope became more of a reality. On my fourth luncheon visit, Alyssa asked me to bring Leo the following week. Leo and I were very close to living together by then, but I'd only told Alyssa about a few dinners and parties we'd attended together. However, Leo's son, Ben, was still her primary care doctor, and I was beginning to believe something more was developing between them—a thought too odd to contemplate. Alyssa always had glowing things to say about Ben each week; he was also a visitor. Apparently Quinton, when I finally questioned her about him, had moved on and was divorcing her. She seemed relieved by that.

On a hot Saturday in July, I drove Leo to Twin Lakes to visit Alyssa. I didn't know why the visit was so fraught with emotion—well, I did, I suppose. I knew she was working out her demons about having abandoned her beloved father while he was sick, so I feared she still thought of Leo as an interloper. She'd improved so much over the past month, I hoped for the best—that word again. Leo and I were unusually quiet for the two-hour drive and spent most of the time listening to a recording of a local jazz group I'd discovered. When I pulled into my usual parking spot, Alyssa, as usual, appeared at my car window.

"Hi, Leo. Welcome to Shangri-La. Just joking." She tittered and rolled her eyes, looking embarrassed. "Come on, you two. Let's get over to lunch."

As we started over to the lunch area, Leo said, "You look fabulous, Alyssa. Your mom told me you've been doing a lot of swimming."

"Yeah. I think I could do a triathlon soon. I've been running too, but no biking yet. I've got Ben to thank for recommending this place. It's been, well, a lifesaver."

"It was a lifesaver for Ben too. I know he's shared that with you."

She looked at the ground. "Uh-huh."

Her neck and face had turned bright pink when Leo mentioned Ben—the thought of mother-daughter, father-son romances made me uncomfortable. We arrived at the buffet—inside this time since the heat was oppressive and air-conditioning was mandatory. Almost everyone there said hi to Alyssa as we passed tables full of chattering, mostly young, people. Alyssa smiled at each hello like the queen of the cafeteria she'd been in high school. She must have been using whitening strips, because her smile was sparkling for the first time in ages. She'd also stopped smoking—hooray.

When we sat down with our plates, she said, "Leo, before I chicken out, uh, I started about three letters to you this past week. I've wanted to thank you, for weeks now, for saving my life." Leo started to reply but she held up her hand. "And, I want to add, I'm really happy you and my mom are happy together."

Leo did his throat-clearing exercise. "And I'm happy you're doing so well. I consider you family now, because your mother is the most important person in my life. And I—" Leo looked close to tears. I'd never seen him quite so overwhelmed.

"So you two," I said. "Let's eat before…I'm hungry as a gator."

Between mouthfuls, Leo said, "Your mother has become a gator aficionado. She's been photographing the one who owns my little lake. I keep a huge rake handy in case I have to beat it off her—he's at least four feet long. But she took some amazing shots and she's entered two in an art contest."

"Cool, Mom, but be careful. Gators still scare me. Our pool is fenced so no gators can get in."

I swallowed some lemonade. "I'm careful but fascinated by them. Maybe I can learn patience from the gators. They lie in the water or sun on the bank for ages, just waiting for a bird or a fish to come close. I made a video of our gator catching an egret, white feathers flying."

"Ew. Ugh, Mom, gross."

"We all need a hobby!" I answered and she laughed.

The luncheon was success, better than I'd expected. On the drive home, Leo was ecstatic about how good Alyssa looked, how happy she'd sounded, and, of course, how pleased she'd seemed to be with Leo. "We're a family now, sweetheart—all the way."

***

I hadn't been to New York City since my horrific trip to Brooklyn to rescue Alyssa. The accommodations were much better—I was staying in a high-ceiling, pre-war apartment on Fifth Avenue. It had a lovely view of Central Park, or would have if it hadn't been raining and flooding throughout the city. Susan was getting married at the Mandarin Oriental, probably the most gorgeous hotel in Manhattan. The night before the wedding we all got soaked getting to a special dinner for the bridal party at the hotel. Alyssa, who'd been back in Brooklyn in a halfway house with four other women for three weeks, looked healthy and beautiful at the dinner—maybe a bit plump due to her bipolar meds. Since she left rehab, she'd been keeping in touch through email and texts almost every day. She was looking for work and already had a few interviews set up for next week. Hope pumped through my body, but I knew there was no guarantee she'd stay off illegal drugs and stay on needed meds. In my brain, my fingers were always crossed, but I kept *hope* alive.

I kissed Leo goodbye as I prepared to go to the Mandarin Oriental where a team of beauty technicians were waiting to work magic on Susan, Alyssa, and me. I gathered up my dress bag and the doorman hailed a cab and held an umbrella over my head till I got in.

Alyssa arrived at the entrance to the Mandarin at the same moment. Staff ushered us inside and led us to a private salon area. Three estheticians from the salon washed and colored our hair, then spent what seemed like hours whipping our hair into new designs. Susan and I had short hair, but they made us look like we had mounds and mounds of it. Alyssa told her technician exactly what she wanted—no frou-frou like us oldies. Susan stated, "Don't make my hair too fat. I just lost weight."

We were offered "healthy" water, snacks, and champagne. After the hair magic, the estheticians put pounds of makeup on each of us. We looked at ourselves and each other in the acres of mirrors.

"Wow. We look damn good!" I blurted out.

Alyssa giggled. "Yeah. You two look like movie stars."

Susan choked on her Evian. "We don't look too shabby, huh."

The beauticians also helped us into our fancy underwear and dresses, fussing with each puff of hair spray, each swipe of lip gloss. Susan had chosen Manhattan for her wedding because she and Michael had relatives and friends there, and most would not travel to Florida even for their own mother's funerals. And August because Michael's son was only free in August.

Fully dressed and prepped, I stared at Alyssa, who looked lovely in her pink bridesmaid dress. I looked ridiculous in the same dress: full length, with ruffles around the boobs, and spaghetti straps. Pink was not my color, but Susan seemed to be having a great laugh at my expense—I'd forced her into an almost identical dress over forty years ago, and it looked truly awful on her short, plump shape.

Today Sue was elegant in a long, low-cut, cream-colored dress with lace sleeves; no veil on her head, just a crown of tiny rosebuds. She'd lost a total of sixty pounds since her diet and exercise and Michael regimen began. Her figure looked like a short Marilyn Monroe, but Sue's cleavage rivaled Marilyn's and she grew in stature when she put on four-inch heels. When she started to practice walking and tottered all around, we knew she'd need us to get her down the aisle safely.

Susan let out one of her huge guffaws. "Well, you two are a pretty in pink! Especially you, Maureen." She couldn't stop laughing. "You ready to walk me down the aisle?"

"Aunt Sue, you look beautiful, y'know?"

"Thanks, honey. And I'm sure glad you're here. You look too gorgeous to walk me down the aisle, but I love ya."

All three of us looked at the top of our game, especially Alyssa, but she was over forty years younger. I took Susan's hand. "Let's go, dear friend, before I start to cry and ruin my professional paint job."

Alyssa and I each took one of her arms and we sidestepped through the door. A bellwoman led us into the elevator and down to the ballroom entrance. We'd started giggling in the elevator and could not stop, but laughing held off the tears I knew I'd shed soon. We stood together at the entrance to a high-ceilinged, sparkling room—about one hundred people were seated, and no one had noticed us except for Michael. The walls shimmered in the light from sconces around the room. When the music started, the traditional wedding march, we three walked down the red carpet together, barely suppressing our laughter. A thinner but still happy-faced

Michael waited by the *huppah* with his two sons by his side: all three of them short and a bit plump, all three wearing blue suits, all three bald. When we made it down the long aisle, Alyssa and I released Susan and she toddled over to Michael.

The smell of freesia perfumed the air. I turned to look at the people in the first row and smiled at Leo. He gave me his big wink and mouthed, "I love you."

Today, I was overflowing with joy.

About the Author

Kathleen McMahon Schwartz began her professional life as a girly geek—mathematics major at SUNY Albany, computer programmer/analyst for AT&T and Honeywell in New York, later a tenured college instructor of Information Systems, then a technical writer for several years at AT&T and IBM. Finally tired of tech, she attended a writing seminar at the Stowe Library in Vermont and was inspired to begin a new career path as a fiction writer. *Stay the Night* is her first novel, and a new romance set in Mexico is underway.

Kathleen and her husband recently traded their ski house in Vermont for a pool house in Florida, where her two sons and five stepsons will be frequent visitors. For fun, she was an improvisational role player for over nine years while in New Jersey, performing with a group of actors in many venues, from PTA groups to corporate training sessions. She is now a puppeteer, using her "granny" puppet to entertain at nursing homes.

Credits

This book is a work of art produced by The Zharmae Publishing Press.

Sara Bangs
Editor-in-Chief

Carrie Hemler
Associate Editor

Star Foos
Designer

Suzanne Spooner & Tiffani Smith
Editorial Contributions

Benjamin Grundy
Typesetter

Olivia Swenson
Proofreader

Ally Boice
Copy Editor

Rachel Garcia & Lori Bartlett
Reader

Randolph Castro,
Reviewer

Edward Mack
Coordinating Producer

Erin Sinclair
Managing Editor

Tomiko Breland
Associate Publisher

Travis Robert Grundy
Publisher

August 2015
The Zharmae Publishing Press